FOREVER CHANGED

JANE CARVER

When you come out of the storm,
you won't be the same person
who walked in.
That's what this storm is all about.

—Haruki Marakami—
Contemporary bestselling author of
The Wind-up Bird Chronicle

TEXAS STRONG

When you pass through the waters,
I will be with you.

ISAIAH 43:2

H urricanes rarely last even forty-eight hours. They churn in warm waters, make landfall, then move on quickly as a rain storm.

Almost exactly one-hundred-twenty-seven years after the great storm hit Galveston, Texas, Hurricane Harvey hit the Texas Gulf coast. The slow-moving hurricane made landfall just north of Corpus Christi, at Rockport, devastating the small town and those near it. The storm then downgraded to a powerful tropical storm and moved inland only a hundred miles to sit and rain for days. It then moved back into the Gulf—all at an excruciatingly slow pace—and pounded the coast up past Victoria, Palacios and the Houston metro area, dropping unprecedented amounts of rain. After six days, it made yet another landfall near the Texas/Louisiana border, but not before turning towns like Beaumont and all the tiny communities around it into virtual islands, inaccessible except by boat.

The damage was unimaginable, but Texans across the state stepped up, even while Harvey dropped enough rain to end the drought in the entire state of California. An unbelievable 50+ inches fell to the east of Houston alone.

While Gulf coast folks rushed to help, we didn't weather this storm alone.

First responders, firemen, police and the National Guard simply couldn't handle the sheer numbers of calls asking for rescue. So, citizens stepped in, bringing boats. Texans from around the state showed up. The 'Cajun Navy' from Louisiana brought their airboats. Other states sent personnel and equipment from as far away as New York, reciprocating after Texas helped them through Hurricane Sandy's recovery.

Through it all—in wind and water—Texans hit the ground even as the rains began, came together, never asking color, religion, gender or status. They helped their neighbors get out safely, then took care of them in shelters. Texans helped when those displaced folks returned to water-damaged homes, moving, ripping, mopping up. Offering hands to help and shoulders to cry on.

We weren't alone. Others helped. Saying 'thank you' just doesn't seem enough.

The immediate aftermath of the great storm of 1900 that devastated Galveston created the first recognized national relief effort by citizens of the United States and even foreign countries. That tradition of helping remains strong today. Not just 'Houston Strong' where the phrase started but Texas Strong because that's who we are...a state—and a nation—of strong caring people.

If some other place needs help after a natural disaster, I know the spirit of helping that abounds in Texas will flow over to those in need.

LIFE IS LOOKIN' GOOD

"That ol' gulf's gonna swaller you up, then spit you out some day if you're not careful, Georgie," I yell to the nine-year-old gallivanting along the water's edge. I speak in my high silly voice that he thinks is funny. Maybe he'll pay attention...this time. Nope, he's still daring waves to reach him without drenching him. The young fella sets me to laughing as he chases waves that swell, race to shore like a wild animal intent on attacking, then peter out, washing ashore as harmless as a wet hankie.

Saturday afternoon, early spring in the island city of Galveston. A perfect day after a winter of more rain than I can remember. Days of cold —not numbing but just miserable cold so as your coat's not thick enough, even for the coastline of Texas. At least Georgie has a place to stay with plenty of food and a warm bed. Does he even have to share it with someone else when he goes to sleep at night like me? I've never asked, and he's never said.

I'm like lots of other fellas. I flop in one room at a house up on 20th street. Three other boys share that room with me. Four bedrooms. Four boys in each. Lots of fellas running around in one widow's weather-beaten house. We pay five cents a week, and that doesn't include anything to eat. The beds squeak, and the sheets only get washed once a month. I'd rather not be there, but I have little choice. Actually, there's no choice. That's just how it is. The past few years haven't been all that good. Here it is—spring of 1899, and life's finally looking up. But I still gotta bed in with strangers.

"Sister's gonna swat his butt if he gets all wet." A tall thin Negro boy stops next to me, his pants legs rolled up and his jacket and hat in hand. He's a quiet soul and good company, a fella used to hard labor.

"Hi, Samuel." Samuel's my best friend. Samuel Houston Perkins, named for one of the great heroes of Texas. He's a dreamer. You listen to him, and you swear he can see into the future. His family—mother, father, three sisters and three brothers—live near the beach on the east end of the island. I envy them. All they have to do is look out the kitchen window and see the gulf waters.

Guess there's a bit of dreamer in me as well sometimes. I want to go to sea. Be a merchant man. Help carry cargo across the oceans. When I was younger—before my maw's death and my paw's...well, leaving, I used to watch the waves and listen to my teacher tell about the great ships riding them in calm and storm.

That was further down the coast, nearer Indianola. That place is gone now. Storm wiped it out, so folks up and moved away. My family— what was left—moved around some before landing here. Often, I ask myself why I've not hitched myself to one of those big cargo ships that tie up at the Galveston docks every day. I remind myself why I shouldn't go...why I can't go. Duty is a heavy burden sometimes.

Samuel chuckles as Georgie runs up and stops by my side so fast he almost spins us around. "That's them," he says, pointing down the beach and ducking behind us.

"Don't be scared of 'em, Georgie. They're nice." I encourage him to step out from behind and stand between Samuel and me. Along the beach comes the man I work for and his family—the Zimmermans.

I've only been there since mid-winter. Mr. Zimmerman insists I call him Mr. Jack like the other workers in the shop. Feels sort of odd, calling a grown-up man by his first name, me being fourteen and all. But he insists. Not mean-like but friendly-like.

Mr. Jack always sends me to the house when he wants something. His furniture workshop is only a block away from the boarding house his wife runs.

Ms. Christie—that's Mr. Jack's wife—sees me and waves. I give her a timid wave. She's an odd one, one-minute bossy and the next as tender as Vassy's fried chicken.

Vassy's the Zimmerman's cook. Mr. Jack invited me to Sunday dinner last week. I hem-hawed around, not really wanting to hobnob with the boarders or embarrass the Zimmermans or myself by showing up in the same clothes I work in. But he mentioned how I might enjoy eating in the big ol' kitchen out behind the main house and keep company with Ms. Vassy and Juliet the little maid. Man-like company, he said with a wink. I took that to mean he was joking about me being a man in a lady's company, but he insisted I come.

So I did. I still dream about Vassy's fried chicken. Maybe Juliet walks through some of those dreams, too, but I don't remember. I feel heat creep up my neck and face, just thinking about the pretty girl. Not that I'm gonna do anything with her, like stepping out or courting.

The Zimmerman children run around their mother and father like whirlwinds—at least the oldest one Jackson, or Jackie as they call him, and his sister Louise—do. The youngest child, a boy named Lawrence, holds his mother's hand. Louise and Lawrence look alike. Mr. Jack said they're twins, born on the same day. He said it kind of quiet, birthing not being something folks talk about out loud.

"Since you're gonna be around the house, you might as well know the lay of the land, young man," he said as he thumped me on the back the first time he sent me running to the house. I could see the back of the house and kitchen from the workshop's front door. "Mind what Ms. Christie tells you to do with this here nightstand." He handed a small cabinet with two drawers to me, the top wrapped in a heavy cloth. "And..." He winked—the man winks a lot. "If you happen through Vassy's kitchen and give her a big grin, she might give you some of that chocolate cake she said she'd be baking for supper tonight." With that, he pushed me out the door.

The man makes me feel...worth something. A feeling I never got from my paw.

Mr. Jack and Jackie play tag as they approach us. Man and boy scamper like puppies around the lady and twins. Jackie is full of piss and vinegar. Daring his father to chase him, snatching his hat up when the wind catches it and lifts it off the man's smooth brown hair. But rather than return it, Jackie, that six-year-old scamp, sets it at a jaunty angle on his small head and gallops toward me, his laughter merry and loud.

A capricious wind tricks the lad by blowing the straw hat off his head, rolling it back toward its owner. Jackie howls, then giggles as he runs to hide behind Samuel and me. He's about the same height as Georgie and uses him as a shield.

"Gather tight, boys. Help me hide from Father," he whispers loud enough for us to hear over the waves rolling in at our feet.

Samuel and I hide our grins and lean against each other. But Mr. Jack's smart. He guesses where his son is hiding. He twists to the left in order to fake out the boy. As Jackie edges the other way—more to my side—Mr. Jack twists back to the right, reaches around and pulls his son out from behind us. Both break into loud laughter, for Mr. Jack is tickling Jackie something unmerciful. Eventually they both collapse into a cackling heap on the sand at our feet.

Three-year-old Louise runs up and jumps on top of both. Mr. Jack's arm comes up and hauls her into the tickling fray. Like puppies wrestling at bedtime, man, boy and girl rustle around in an undignified romp.

"Look at the sand I'm going to have to sweep up when we get home, Lawrence." Ms. Christie and her youngest son come to a stop beside Samuel, unmindful it appears, or uncaring, that he's a black boy. The beach seems to be a great equalizer. "Hard to tell man from child down there, isn't it," she tosses companionably to the three of us, never taking her eyes off the trio rolling around on the sand.

"Afternoon, Jonathan. I see you have the same idea we did...enjoy this lovely weather." She nods to me, then to Samuel and Georgie. "And who are these gentlemen?"

"This is Samuel Houston Perkins, ma'am," I introduce Samuel who gets all big-eyed at being noticed by a white lady.

Ms. Christie pays no attention to his skin color. She holds out her hand, never letting go of Lawrence's small hand. "Nice to meet you, Mr. Perkins. Named after the great General Sam Houston, I presume?"

"Uh, ma'am. I mean..." Samuel stutters but manages to finish his sentence. "That is, yes, ma'am. General Sam Houston." Panic leaves his face, replaced by pride.

"I'm sure you'll live up to your namesake, Mr. Perkins." She leans forward a bit, the better to see Georgie, once more hiding at my side.

"And this fine fella is?"

"Uh..." Now I'm at a loss how to explain Georgie.

"I'm Georgie. Jonathan's best friend," he pipes up, then quickly adds, "Ma'am" as he steps out from my side and offers his salty hand. I try to swap it back to my side, but too late. Ms. Christie has taken his hand and given him a solemn shake.

"Best friends are hard to find. Best Jonathan remembers his." She nods once more, a habit I noticed early on. Mr. Jack winks; Ms. Christie nods. Peculiar. No stranger than my silly voice, I suppose.

The youngest boy, Lawrence, says nothing the entire time. I can't remember ever hearing him talk. But his eyes haunt you once you've looked into them. The little fella reminds me of Samuel; he sees more than most. Perhaps even into a soul.

A shiver rattles up my back. I look away from the little guy and back to those three, rough housing on the sand. I like boys like this one—Jackie. Full of life and good cheer. Willing to try anything. Go anywhere. Have adventures. Mr. Jack and Jackie took off several times during the winter months to deliver pieces of furniture that the workshop makes by hand. Going across town to Avenue J—what folks in Galveston call Broadway. Going on to Market, Mechanic and the Strand—streets bustling with activity. Seeing shops and visiting with those who know the Zimmerman family. While the boy Lawrence stays inside, settled and quiet, Jackie is an outside boy like me, ready for anything. Ready to go adventuring.

Toward us come two I recognize—Juliet the maid and Vassy the cook.

7

Between them, they carry a huge picnic basket. Each one carries a blanket over her arm. Looks like the family plans a picnic on the beach. Maybe they're as tired of being cooped up inside as my friends and I are.

For the first time, I notice that Ms. Christie and young Louise wear bathing costumes. Ladies wear a shorter dress with those cap things that cover their hair when they swim. Naw, they don't really swim; they wade. Dip their toes into the water, squeal and run back to dry land. Silly but it's fun watching their antics.

"Seems like it's time to get this bunch up and dusted off. Lawrence, you find us a nice spot to settle onto and ask Vassy and Juliet to set up our lunch there. I'll be along presently as soon as I get your father and these two hooligans up." With that, she waves him off, scoots past Samuel and me and reaches down to yank up Louise by the back of her bathing costume. That young lady comes up sputtering. Her mother pulled the collar a bit tight and almost choked the kid.

Samuel and I hid our grins behind our hands. No telling what that brown-haired whirlwind would do if she heard us laughing at her. Three she might be, but she's a fierce one.

"Louise Marie Zimmerman, brush yourself off, and march over there with your brother this instant," Ms. Christie commands. As her daughter passes, dusting and grumbling, the mother swats her bottom. "And watch what you say. I can hear you." Louise immediately shuts up. "That girl wears out more clothes than any boy I have," she comments to us, giving her head a decided jerk for emphasis.

By that time, both Mr. Jack and Jackie sit on the sand, side-by-side, clothes in disarray, hair standing straight up on Mr. Jack's head, while Jackie's slightly longer hair is twisted around like a strong wind has gotten hold of it.

"Really! You two are impossible." Ms. Christie gives up trying to settle the giggles that still vibrate between son and father. "Gentlemen," she addresses Samuel, Georgie and me. "These two aren't in any condition to join us for a meal. Would you like to share with us? God knows Vassy cooked for two days in preparation for this outing."

"But Ms.—" I begin. The three of us aren't quality folks. We're poor hands that are fortunate enough to earn a bit of coin. Well, Samuel and I are. Georgie helps out around the orphanage, though he's not really an orphan. Sister and him have an agreement of a kind…he works for her, and she feeds him and lets him flop downstairs. I don't know all the arrangements they agreed to, and they're an odd pair. But she takes care of him, and he does right by her. If it works, then I'm all for staying out of their business.

"Ms. Christie," I try again. "We're not for polite society," I whisper, embarrassed I have to remind her. The Zimmermans have the oddest way about them when it comes to common folk. They just don't see a difference. But I do. And Samuel and Georgie do, too.

"Gentlemen, even if these two manage to meet us there in time and in better condition, you are still invited to join us." Ms. Christie nods her head with a jerk once more, then proceeds to turn her back on us. Not ignoring us but as if she expects us to follow.

"Like she says, boys, you've been invited." Mr. Jack rises beside us, swatting his own stripped body bathing suit. Jackie hands him the straw hat that began the wrestling match. The man settles the hat on his head, then holds out a hand, gesturing for us to lead the way.

"But Mr. Jack, we ain't fit company—" I try again before even he cuts me off.

"You work for me. These young fellas are your friends. It's a perfect day for family and friends to unite over a good meal. And Vassy cooks good meals. Am I right, Jonathan?"

He has me there. Vassy is one in a million when it comes to food.

I give in. "Yes, sir. Ms. Vassy can cook for St. Peter and greet all the newcomers to heaven with her fried chicken."

"There you have it, gentlemen. Time to eat. You first."

Samuel, however, backs up. "Thank you kindly, sir. But I think my mama might be looking for me." He keeps backing up, giving me and Georgie a casual wave. "Thanks for asking, Mr. Zimmerman." Without further word, he turns and breaks into a run. Before long, he disappears into the crowd that covers the beach today.

Mr. Jack sighs. "I wish it were otherwise. We fought a war in order to sit at the same table and share a meal. We've got so far to go yet." He nods toward the blankets and picnic hampers. "Let's eat."

I glance sideways at Georgie. His mouth practically drools over the food laid out. I'm not sure when Sister will pick him up. I'm not sure if his supper that night will be as good as even the smallest portion of the Zimmerman's feast. I'm not sure if joining them is the right thing to do or not.

Before I can change my mind, I thump the young fella between the shoulder blades and get him moving toward the fun and feast. "No sense going hungry when we're invited," I squeak in my silly voice. That's all the encouragement Georgie needs.

Pretty soon the lot of us sit like Indians at peace talks—that's something else my teacher taught us—how to sit cross legged. Perhaps Ms. Christie anticipated meeting friends on the beach. Perhaps Vassy always packs too many plates and forks. But we each had a plate full of food and a fork to eat with. I'm not sure how Georgie feels, but for a minute, I feel like part of something bigger than me. A family maybe. But mine never felt like this. Not really.

Before morbid thoughts steal my pleasure, I hear Sister calling Georgie. The little guy's never told me Sister's name. The Catholic sisters that run the orphanage always go by Sister something. But Georgie just calls this one Sister. Together they ride the buggy into town for supplies. Often, she lets Georgie play on the beach while she buys what's needed for the day and waits for it to be loaded. She often visits Mother Superior—that's the head of the nuns here on the island. That gives Georgie more time to play. I often meet him for a few minutes. He's a nice little boy. Sister tells him that, and he's quick to tell me what she says. Not real humble of him, but then he's young yet.

With his mouth full of pie, Georgie swipes his face with a napkin, scattering crumbs down onto his shirt. "Fank few, mu'um," he manages before he swats me on the back of the head and scampers across the sand toward the buggy.

"I think he means 'thank you, ma'am'," I add in a hurry. I don't want anyone to be offended.

"I'm pretty sure I've heard something like that before from one of my own sons," Ms. Christie says as her eyebrows lift, and her gaze glances at Jackie. "I guess that head slap is his way of telling you goodbye, yes?"

"Yes, ma'am. He's never been one for goodbyes. That's about as good as it gets for Georgie."

"Cute child," she adds as she counts her own three. Not a big family but for a mother who's as busy as she is running a boarding house filled with men from various jobs, coming and going at all times of the day and night, day in and day out, she already has her hands full.

I doubt her children fear what I do. I doubt they'll ever discover their life is a lie, a life to be thrown away without a second thought, like mine. I doubt they seek happiness because they are happy now. What more can they ask for?

"Jonathan, would you pass the pie, please?" Ms. Christie holds out her hand for the dish without even glancing my way.

Does she trust me to hand over the treat without breaking the precious dish that contains it? My mind flashes to a platter Paw bought for Maw when I was a little shaver. At supper one night, Maw asked me to pass that platter. Paw had killed a rabbit that day, and Maw stewed it up with vegetables from her garden. All that food mounded up on that dish made my mouth water. Maw asking me to pass it from one side of me to the other and hand it over to her left me quivering though. What if...?

What if happened. I was so nervous I tipped the platter. All that meat and those tender vegetables slid off and made a soft wet plopping sound as it hit the wooden planks of the floor. Paw roared up out of his chair, aimed a meaty fist for my head but hit Maw's special platter instead. Like a rock sent sailing out over the gulf water, that dish sailed through the cabin to crash into a hundred pieces against the wall. My heart broke into as many pieces. My fault—that was my fault. The food. The platter that Maw loved. The one she only brought out on special occasions. All my fault. Paw agreed. Despite Maw's plea that I was too little to know what happened, Paw belted me until I couldn't stand. Three days I walked like an old man, bent over, in pain. Maw cried for more days than that.

"Jonathan? The pie?" Ms. Christie gives me a look that wants to know what I'm thinking. I shake my head, not willing to share my thoughts with anyone, much less a family that treats me so fairly. I gather the pie plate in both hands and move it swiftly but carefully into hers.

"Thank you, sir," she says before setting it down to dish out a slice for Mr. Jack and Lawrence.

Vassy, Juliet and I sit at the edge of the second blanket. But that touches the first one where the family sits. Almost as if we're an extension. I see how valuable the cook and maid are to the Zimmermans. But me? I'm nobody. Just an errand boy and a clean-up boy in the shop. Still I look around and see smiles. Mine included. If only for a little time, it's nice to be wanted.

"Hey, Jonathan!" Someone shouts my name from down the beach. I barely hear it.

"More friends of yours, Jonathan?" Mr. Jack shades his eyes and notes the two boys moving toward us.

I glance over my shoulder and give a silent groan. Rowdy and Jason aren't as couth as Samuel or even Georgie. I leave myself out of the equation. These two run about Galveston picking up whatever odd jobs they can find. Days on end, they have little to do but harass merchants and snitch smokes off unsuspecting shopkeepers.

"Hey, Jon, we got your smokes," Rowdy shouts before he's even close enough for me to see he's been snitching more than cigarettes. With one hand, he waves those smokes; with the other hand, he waves a dark flask. Looks like he might have snitched a drink or two from the lady that owns the house we share.

"I gotta talk to them. Maybe I best go with them. It's getting late, and we're expected at the house where we live before dark." I carefully unfold my legs and get up without dusting the blanket with any more sand. Georgie already contributed enough sand and crumbs to the poor thing. The laundry where Ms. Christie sends her sheets, blankets and clothes will have a fit getting out the sand and stains we've left behind.

"See you at work Monday, Jonathan?"

"Yes, sir. Bright and early," I reply, edging away to meet the two fellas before they get much closer.

"And who are those ruffians?" comes a voice from behind me.

Mr. Lazarus Winslow—the accountant that sits in a cubicle at Mr. Jack's shop all day, keeping track of who comes and goes, who works or slacks, what each man works on and how much his paycheck will be each Friday. A despicable man. A wolf hiding in sheep's clothing my maw would have said. To Mr. Jack's face, Mr. Winslow acts humble and courteous. Behind his back, Winslow brags of his position and is merciless in his actions toward others. He all but blackmails the workers, daring them to say anything. If so, he'll find some reason to have them fired or short them on wages. I've heard that from several of the men. Winslow's never approached me. Not yet at least. I guess he thinks I'm not important enough.

I followed him one day just to see if he had a family or friends. He walked alone along Avenue M behind the shop and down the street from the boarding house on Avenue L. Once near the east end of the city, he began weaving his way through alleys and onto rougher streets. I lost him there, never knowing where he ended up.

He treats others like ruffians when Mr. Jack isn't looking, but because he controls the paychecks, no one bucks him. And he has the balls to call these chaps 'ruffians'?

"Acquaintances of Jonathan's. How are you, Lazarus?" Mr. Jack gives Winslow a short answer, then distracts him as I move away.

"Thanks, Ms. Christie. I can't remember the last time I had such a meal." I give Vassy a sketch of a bow. "Ms. Vassy. I..." I have no words for a woman who can fill my stomach with such pleasure.

"Hey, Jon. What's going on? Who're these swells?" Jason's whisper isn't as quiet as he thinks. My face blazes with hot embarrassment. The two fellas are closer than I thought.

"See y'all later," I tell the Zimmermans as I take Rowdy and Jason each by an arm and turn them back up the beach.

"Good! Haul that beach trash away from here," Winslow manages to whisper in my ear before I can clear us away from the family.

I shoot a hot glare at him, but it has no more effect than tossing a cup of water into the gulf. He brushes my feelings aside like swatting a mosquito.

"Come on, fellas. Let's get outta here." We get far enough away that I no longer hear that spiteful man accepting Ms. Christie's offer of pie and lemonade. The lanky fella has the gall to fold himself up and collapse in the exact spot where I sat minutes ago.

"Grrr!" My teeth grind together. "Give me over a smoke, will ya?" Taking the rolled smoke, I snatch a Lucifer from Jason and light up. A deep breath and a long pull of smoke, then out into the afternoon's breeze, calms me.

The only thing my paw ever encouraged was my smoking. Maw cried and begged me to stop, saying it was a nasty habit. But Paw feinted a punch to her face that she ducked, and she never mentioned my smoking again. For her I might have stopped, but Paw kept offering—insisting—and after a while that was how I calmed myself—with a puff of ta'bacci.

The more I think about Winslow in the middle of that nice family the more I think of a snake slithering out of the vines along the sand dunes and into an innocent heart.

"Have a swig, Jon," Jason offers. He passes a flask to me, making sure the sleeve of his jacket hides it.

"Where'd you get this?" Upset at how a nice adventure has turned into such an unhappy ending, I throw back a deep swallow and end up coughing my lungs out for a good minute or so.

"That'll teach you. Gotta sip this smooth stuff slow." Rowdy sips from the flask, then thumps the cork back in place. "I'll fill it up when we get home and put it back on Mrs. Abby's sideboard. She'll never miss it."

Once a proud woman with a large house, Mrs. Abby now has no husband and no money but what the boys pay her for a week's worth of bedding. Her only solace is that whiskey Rowdy snitched from her.

Wrong to take it or not, today I need that drink more than she does. We find a shady place under a pier and lean back against the piling. Until it's empty, we pass around the flask and talk about the folks we see around us. Inventing stories as they suit us. I entertain the two with my impressions.

"All gone," Rowdy points out as he tips up the flask. Not a drop falls from the open end.

"Shoot. Guess there's nothing to do but find something to eat and head home." Jason stands, pulling Rowdy up first, then me. He scratches his rear end and picks his nose. "I'll make a swing by the bakery and see if there's any day-old bread to be had. Rowdy, you head over to the grocery and get us something to add to that." Meaning steal something while an unsuspecting shopper hides his activity.

"Jon, you—"

"Look, guys. I'm good for tonight. I think I'll head home." Home... Mrs. Abby's shabby house with dirty sheets and two to a bed. I shudder, thinking of Georgie in his warm bed, maybe alone and the Zimmerman children in rooms of their own. Not sharing space, sheets or beds.

Depressed now, I leave my companions, wishing I could go back to the beach and maybe find Samuel or... But with Winslow there, I'd not be welcomed to rejoin the Zimmermans.

One thought gives me hope for tomorrow though. I'll be back with Mr. Jack and maybe run more errands in the fine spring weather. With any luck, as usual, I'll avoid the accountant. That thought alone sends a grin to my face and adds spirit to my step.

———

"Willie?" Mrs. Abby greets me as I enter the kitchen door.

"No, ma'am. It's me—Jonathan."

"Oh, dear. You and Willie look so much alike—tall, green eyes and that hair that always looks like it needs a good trimming." The old lady sighs. She's old but not blind. Just gets me and the boy in the next bed mixed up now and then. Each room has two beds. Two boys in each. Jason and I share one bed. Rowdy and Willie share the other. Willie works at a green grocery closer to the middle of town. He often supplies fruit for supper.

"You in for the night, dear?" The old lady likes to think of us as her children rather than boarders.

"Yes, ma'am."

"Did you eat?"

"I had something with friends. The family I work for showed up at the beach, and they gave me something to eat."

"Well, if you get hungry, you let me know. But we'll keep that to ourselves, won't we, dear."

She's got a kind heart. Before I started working for Mr. Jack, I did odd jobs for her. She paid me in meals. She said I was nice to her. The other boys sometimes make fun of her. So, we keep these handouts a secret.

"Be sure to wash up if you've been on the beach all day," she reminds me. She tells all the boys that every night. We lot work various jobs, and some of the lads are dirtier than others. No one wants to sleep with a guy who stinks. Funny how Mrs. Abbey's such a stickler for washing bodies but not for washing sheets more often.

———

Jason tosses a wad of greens on the bed, while Rowdy breaks apart a stale loaf of bread. The bread still smells fresh though. The greens are long past fresh. I'll have no part of them, but a bit of bread to gnaw on wouldn't be amiss.

"You like working for those folks, Jon?" Jason leans back on the bed, finishing a bread and greens sandwich he created.

"Sure. They're nice enough. They pay me regular and don't have lots of rules." I've taken off my shoes, socks, trousers and shirt. I passed a wet rag over my face and chest earlier before they came in. Washing the salt water and sand off my arms and hands helps settle me for sleep. First one to sleep don't hear the others snore. I lay under the dingy sheet, my head propped on my arm, atop a meager pile of feathers Mrs. Abbey calls a pillow.

Rowdy pulls out a smoke and lights up. He passes it among the three of us. Just as the last of it burns out, Willie slithers through the door.

He's about our age but has seen more of the world than the three of us together. He sailed for a bit until the captain threw him off for stealing. He worked the docks but got tossed for picking pockets. Yet his smooth tongue kept him out of the hands of the police each time. I have little truck with him. I leave him alone; he leaves me alone. We simply share a bedroom. At times, I don't envy Rowdy his sleeping companion. Willie works the fishing wharves now and then. On those days, he comes into the room smelling like the bottom of Galveston bay. The guy doesn't know what soap and water are.

"You lot out and about today? Get anything interesting?" Willie pulls off his clothes in a fashion resembling a whirlwind. The dirty pieces fall into a heap on the floor. He gives a backward hop and throws himself onto the bed. The springs under the thin mattress screech in protest. He ignores the possibility of his bed collapsing.

"We don't go in for your kind of activities," Jason says as he shucks off his clothes but manages to hang them over mine on the chair back beside our bed.

As Rowdy undresses, he and I remain silent. No sense in sounding better than the fourth member of this room. Life might get intolerable otherwise.

"Anyone got another smoke?" Willie asks. "I'm fresh out."

The three of us have a smoke apiece left but don't offer him any. "Sorry. Fresh out," I lie and roll over with my back to him and the room.

Jason settles on his side of our bed. Amazing how two fellas can sleep soundly yet hug the edge of a mattress. "Go to sleep, will ya, Willie. We got things to do tomorrow."

Rowdy blows out the candle in the tall hurricane lamp on the dresser. Mrs. Abbey can no longer afford the electric lights she once used when her husband was alive.

"Naw, you fellas got nothing more to do tomorrow than me. 'Cept Jon there. He works for that German family. Bet he gets fat eating all that kraut. Then again, they may not work him on Sunday. What do ya say, Jon?"

I can hear Willie holding his breath. I can almost read his mind. Wondering if I'll take the bait he tossed out.

I ignore him. Getting tossed out of Mrs. Abbey's house for fighting isn't worth it. We already tread on quicksand by smoking in the room. The house is old and threadbare. Mrs. Abbey constantly worries about fires. Does she pay fire insurance? Will the firemen save her house if she don't? I'm not sure how that works, but Rowdy, Jason and I long ago made a pact among ourselves that—at least in this case—we'll be careful, so as not to lose a place to flop at night. Sleeping outdoors during nice weather is okay, but rain and cold makes for a miserable night. I know; I've been in that situation. So, we do the quiet but dangerous smoking while avoiding if possible the noisy but less dangerous fighting. My life is riddled with lies. What's one more?

———

Next morning being Sunday, I have no place I have to be, but I'm not sticking around with these guys any longer than I have to. Mr. Johnson at the green grocery near the boarding house gave me coins for the paper check Mr. Winslow begrudgingly gave me on Friday. Old man Johnson holds it for me; I trust him. I take a few coins to use on Sunday because I have no place to get a meal. Georgie and Samuel are doing the church thing.

I admit at times I sit outside the German church and listen to the singing, but no one's getting me inside to listen to a bunch of words about God loving me and giving me a good life, then sending me to Heaven. There's no such thing as a good life. My maw and little sister, born dead, might be in a place called Heaven, but me? Naw, Heaven's not waiting for me. I got big dreams, but the truth is, I got no way to make them happen. So, God ain't part of my plans. The singing though—that's okay.

Somehow, my feet take me in the direction of the Zimmerman boarding house. I sit under a window beside the dining room. A brick walkway passes from the tall front porch, down the side of the house into a small back yard. On the far side is the outbuilding where Vassy creates those wonderful meals. My mouth waters thinking about what the boarders are having this morning.

I enjoy sitting on the iron bench tucked into the oleanders. My stomach growls, but I try to ignore it. Not easy when my last meal was mid-day the day before. Oh, that and a bite of bread.

"Ms. Christie, I've a big spoonful of oatmeal left over and the heels of that loaf of bread them boarders just finished. What do you want me to do with that bit? Not enough to feed any of these men, but too much to toss to the chickens. Besides, I doubt chickens eat oatmeal. Especially with a touch of brown sugar I added." Vassy moves away from the window.

My sigh can be heard for a mile, I suspect. At least I think that's what Ms. Christie might have heard. She sticks her head out the window across from me, shaking crumbs from a napkin.

"Jonathan! Imagine seeing you here." Her grin lifts my spirits. "Jonathan, can you help Vassy with a problem? I'm sure you've already eaten, but she's got a spoonful or two of oatmeal and a few slices of bread that no one's going to eat. Do you think you might force yourself to eat it, so she doesn't get unhappy about wasting food?"

She barely gives me time to concoct a story about eating. Withdrawing her head, she flaps the napkin one more time, one hand out the window, then turns all bossy. "Get on with you now, young man. Time and good food's wasting." Just like that, she's gone.

I rise, take two steps toward the front porch, ready to run, but a soft voice behind me stops me like a brick wall.

"Ms. Christie said breakfast is waiting for you in Ms. Vassy's kitchen. Best come on while it's hot." Juliet delivers her message, then turns toward the kitchen, but she stops, glances over her shoulder and says in a much nicer tone than Ms. Christie, "Get on with you now." And she smiles. Jesus! That smile haunts my dreams now and then. How can I ignore an invitation like that? A voice like that? A smile like that?

Like a puppy, I follow the maid into a kitchen so clean I could eat off the floor though thankfully Ms. Vassy points to a chair at the center counter. The smells of cinnamon and fresh bread fill the air. My mouth fills with spit at the idea of eating. A bowl of oatmeal, a glass of milk and a plate with bread already buttered waits—for me. I'm having trouble believing my good luck. I know my best friends are eating well. At least I hope they are. As for Rowdy, Jason and Willie...they can eat what they can get their hands on. Me? I'm not so picky or proud.

I sit myself at that high counter and eat...slowly so as not to look like I'm starving. One more thought of Heaven passes through my mind. I might not make it there, but for sure Ms. Vassy is going to be there cooking for them angels one day.

———

Monday morning, I arrive at the Zimmerman Furniture Factory and report to Mr. Jack himself. "Ready, sir."

"Ah, Jonathan, the very man I need. I've got a table that needs delivering right away. The lady who commissioned it is anxious to get it in place in her business." He winks. He moves to a corner where a small table stands, maybe as tall as my upper leg. The top isn't large around but oddly shaped. At least what I can see of it. An oilcloth covers the top. Below the top is a small shelf supported by four thin legs. The dark wood gleams in the spring sunshine coming through the window directly above us. He hands me a small sack that rattles like it's full of loose change, or in this case, loose wooden pieces from the sounds of it.

Will I be riding in the buggy somewhere or perhaps the large wagon? Naw, this piece isn't big enough for that. I sigh, hoping the job will take me some place interesting.

Mr. Jack snaps my attention back where it belongs—on this delivery job. "Here's the piece. Not too heavy for a strapping lad like you. Here's the checkers. Mind you, don't lose any of these. I made this set myself along with the checker table there on your shoulder. Here's the address." He hands me a paper, the sort that the deliverymen have when making rounds, doling out the goods from the factory.

I give it a good study, hoping I won't have to look at the map in his office to locate the business. With a snort and a wrinkle of my nose, I give him a suspicious glare. "Mr. Jack, this is the address of your home."

"It is?" he asks, quite innocent looking. "Well, I'll be darned. Guess that means the piece Ms. Christie commissioned me to do is finished and ready to be delivered." He slaps me on the shoulder and guides me to the door. "Make sure she signs for the delivery now. We don't want Mr. Winslow to get his sails twisted when a piece is delivered but not signed for."

"No, sir," I grumble as I head out the door and across the street. The boarding house sits at the opposite end of the block. The delivery won't take long. Just get Ms. Christie to sign the paper and I'm back to work in the factory. Even as I think about that, I know curls of wood shavings are piling up under the men's workstations.

If I'm lucky though, I might catch a peak of Juliet.

Go in the front door or the back? Humm. As a businessman, I should go through the front. Especially as this is a commissioned piece.

I walk the path beside the house, past the bench I sat on only yesterday. Up the tall front steps I go, careful not to bump the small table into anything. The homes in Galveston are built high off the ground, so storm waters can flow right under and not damage the houses. Today those tall steps slow me down—but only a little.

I knock on the door and grin when Juliet answers. "I've got something for Ms. Christie. Mr. Jack said she's gotta sign for it though."

"Is that the checker table? She's waited a long time for it. She'll be excited. But..." Juliet stops and glances over her shoulder to the staircase leading up to the family's rooms. "Today Ms. Christie's not feeling well. She was sick this morning."

Folks getting sick ain't a good thing at any time. On an island, even one as close as we are to the coast, sick means getting more doctors if needed. Like an epidemic. I'm too young to remember the influenza epidemic that hit everywhere about the time I was a little shaver. My maw told me so many of her friends died she just stayed home and hugged me hard, hoping we'd be safe. Paw rarely spoke of the sickness, only to say that he saw more dead during that time and helped bury more than he ever wanted to remember.

"Is she real sick?" I want to know.

"Naw, she's just sick in the morning. Been throwing up the past few days. Vassy says she's gonna have a baby." Juliet looks a bit confused. Maybe she's never been around a lady in that condition. I have.

I remember Maw like that when she was going to have that last baby, the one that killed her. Sick every morning, then a few bites of bread and sips of tea, and she'd be right as rain. Pretty soon, the sickness passed, and every bit of her filled with energy. Most amazing thing I ever saw, even though Paw and I never talked about it.

"Ms. Christie's strong for such a scrawny lady. She'll be all right. She's already got three kids though. And all these folks staying here." Speaking of which, I step aside as two railroad men come down the hall, headed for the door.

"Goodbye, Mr. McGraw...Mr. Thrill," Juliet says as she opens the door for them.

"Have a good day, little lady. We'll be back tomorrow. Train will spend the night in Houston, and we'll be picking up cargo as well as passengers. Do let Ms. Vassy know, so she'll not cook too much. But I look forward to her delicious meal when I return." Mr. McGraw, the first man out the door, waves.

Mr. Thrill stops long enough to chunk Juliet under the chin. She doesn't pull back, and she makes no face at him touching her. But by the way she stiffens, I'd be willing to bet she didn't like it.

"He do that all the time?" I can't help asking.

"Too often if you ask me. Mr. Christie usually takes care of the boarders, while I take care of the rooms, but today..." She closes the door and heads to the parlor, a room that all boarders can use.

"Yep, today Ms. Christie's not well." I hate seeing a man touch Juliet. Just seems wrong.

"Place the table here. Do you have the checkers?" she asks as she whisks the oilcloth off the top.

"Wow, would you look at that?" I absentmindedly hand over the bag of what I now know are checkers and squat with hands on knees to inspect the tabletop. Every checker table I've ever seen is a board painted with black and red squares. The checkers are nothing but round pieces of wood. This top is wood but no paint. The light and dark squares are different shades of wood. Mr. Jack can tell me which ones when I return to the shop. The piece is impressive. Each square lies neatly in a hole cut to fit. Light and dark wood fits together around the scrolled top, too. As I admire the tabletop, Juliet places the checkers on top.

Those are even more impressive. Each one has been hand carved. I want to learn how to do that. Carving would be a restful pastime on a merchant ship.

"That's a beaut if ever I saw one," I say sorta low-like.

Juliet seems to agree with me. We stand silently gazing at the small table tucked to one side of the room, between two comfortable-looking chairs. I can imagine two boarders sitting there, smoking their pipes, thinking out each move.

"That's a good idea...that table," I admit.

"Ms. Christie thought so, too. It's taken Mr. Jack an awful long time to get 'er made though." Juliet holds out her hand. "You got a paper. That for Ms. Christie?"

"Yep, but I have to take it back to Mr. Jack, so Mr. Winslow can file it. Ms. Christie needs to sign it."

"That seems silly. She's his wife." Juliet folds her arms across her nicely formed chest and lets her braid fall into her hand. She smoothes the end of the braid as she frowns at me.

"Listen, I'm just the delivery boy, doing what I'm told. Mr. Jack says she needs to sign. It's a business deal, not a husband and wife deal, see."

"I don't know," Juliet hedges around, twisting the braid faster. "I don't want to wake her if she's resting."

"If who's resting?" A voice comes from above us, at the top of the stairs.

"You feeling better, ma'am?" Juliet's grin breaks out like sunshine after a storm. That frantic hair twisting settles into calm hands tucked into her apron pockets.

"Yes, Juliet. I am. Just a bit of upset stomach. It passed." Ms. Christie waves off the morning sickness that expecting ladies get. The topic isn't one folks talk about, but it's nice to know what's going on. Having a baby is a darn sight better than having influenza.

Ms. Christie comes down the stairs slowly, tucking a strand of hair back behind her ear. Her hair rides in a soft bun atop her head, the front of her hair parted. Her blouse has a touch of lace on it and is tucked neatly into a brown skirt. Some sort of flower pin holds the top of her blouse together at the neck. All told, she's a slender lady that often confuses me when she goes from tender to army-tough.

"Ma'am, that checker table finally came," Juliet offers, the silence between the three of us lasting just a beat too long, in my opinion.

"Has it now?" She whirls from the last step and heads into the parlor. With its fourteen-foot ceiling and colored wallpaper, the room appeals to me. Maybe it's just in contrast to the dingy darkness of Mrs. Abbey's home.

"Oh my!" Ms. Christie seems taken aback by the beauty of the little table. Maybe she didn't expect anything so handsome. "Mr. Jack outdid himself this time, children." She runs her hand over the smooth top, then down the narrow dark legs. Of course, I can't say the word 'legs' if we talk about the table. That's not mentioned. I have to say 'supports'. Silly, but I'm not the one making the rules.

"Ms. Christie," I pull the paper out from behind my leg and slide it on top of the table. "Mr. Jack said this is a business deal, and he wants you to sign this paper." I can feel a fidget coming on, worrying about how she'll react to my request.

"He does, does he?" She should be frowning, but instead she stands there with a silly grin on her face. "I do so love that man, you know," she says unexpectedly. Snatching the paper off the checker table, she moves to the writing desk on the far side of the room, sits and pulls a pen to her. With an exaggerated flourish, she signs the paper and hands it over to me. "There you go, sir. Sign, sealed and delivered by one Jonathan Evans to Christie Zimmerman." She stands and pats my shoulder. "On your way back to the shop, why not stop by the kitchen, and see what's for lunch."

"Miss Juliet, you and I have sheets to pull and replace." Just like that, the lady bursts into activity and sends me back to work. By way of Ms. Vassy's kitchen though. My mouth waters when I head for the back screen door.

———

By the end of each day, piles of shavings lay mounded up at the shop's back door. I use a shovel to scoop the mess up into a wagon bed. Tomorrow Michel will drive the shavings to the burn pile outside town.

Though I can't see the beach or gulf from the shop, I can see the colors that streak the evening sky. Light clouds stretch out over the gulf, lit in pink, gold and blue. I lean against my broom handle and admire the show until the light fades enough to turn the clouds a faded gray. Time's passing, and I'll be shoveling these shavings in the dark if I don't get busy.

Inside, a light still burns in Mr. Winslow's office. Paychecks are due out tomorrow. I avoid the man as much as possible. I feel sorry for Juliet— well, and Ms. Christie and Vassy too—because Lazarus Winslow boards at the Zimmerman's place.

He's a smart man, I'll give him that. But by the way he treats the men here, I'd say he lies for his own benefit. He's a judgmental bully. Mr. Jack can't see it. Or won't. Naw, Mr. Jack is a good man and would never allow some snake like Winslow to bully and blackmail his workers. The accountant's idea of violence is intimidation and maneuvering others to do his bidding. Michel told me early on that Winslow took a dislike to a worker named Clarence. Michel never knew what the beef was about, but Winslow hounded the man behind Mr. Jack's back, docked his wages and threatened his family.

"For the pleasure of it all," Michel said.

When Clarence's youngest son was found trampled by a horse in an alley where the child should never have been, Clarence went after Winslow. Not knowing the history between the two, the police found Winslow not guilty when he shot Clarence and acted innocent about why the man came after him. One glaring look from the accountant kept the other workers quiet. Since that time, no one bucks the man who controls the money, though the man who owns the shop is as good as gold but who has no idea a snake hides in that office.

———

Summer passes too quickly, hot as it is.

One thing I discover is that Ms. Christie has a way with weather. She stands on the porch and gazes out, sometimes reaching out. Takes a deep breath. Once in a while she asks me to drive her in the buggy to the beach. Old Gerty doesn't like pulling the buggy through soft sand, so we always stop back from the water's edge on packed sand that probably resembles firmer land to the horse.

Ms. Christie told me the first pass of cold weather—unusual for late September—would blast in for a few days, then we'd settle back to those see-saw hot and chilly days that I'm used to this close to the gulf. Sure enough, two days later, I had to reach for my jacket—one Mr. Jack 'found' in the workshop. Said it was too small for anyone else. That I might as well keep it. A few days after that, I hung it back on a peg near his office. My spot, as he calls it.

I'm a regular at the Zimmerman home each day. Mr. Jack finds all kinds of excuses to send me there, though he's also teaching me how to make furniture. Sometimes I wonder if he's taking pity on me. Other times I'm thankful that a man with his talent for woodworking has taken me on.

Zimmerman's Furniture Factory isn't like those big places with all the machines. All the furniture here is handmade. Any added designs are carved with chisels. The smooth finish shows how much work goes into each piece. I help Mr. Jack deliver pieces. He gave me a shirt to wear one day while we delivered. Said the one I was wearing had sawdust all over it. The shirt had more than sawdust; I'd worn it three days in a row. When we returned, he told me to keep it. Wear it when we were out on business. That, too, hangs on a peg in my spot along the workshop wall.

Sometimes when I change from my sweat-soaked work shirt to that delivery shirt, I hold the thing to my nose, absorb the smell of wood, fresh and clean. Times like that make me feel good.

As fall seeps in, days alternating between hot and cool like some fickled filly, I watch Ms. Christie getting rounder in the middle. The woman never stops though. Jackie has returned to school, but Louise and Lawrence are too young yet to attend classes. I doubt Lawrence is a bother, but I've seen Miss Louise running through the house, like an uncontrolled whirlwind. Her mama or Juliet often guide her back upstairs to the room she shares with her brother, but I doubt she stays there long.

"Really! That child!" Ms. Christie says one day when I bring in the laundry from the wagon stopped by the back gate. Louise is hanging on the side of the laundry wagon, chattering like a bird. "Louise Zimmerman, get over here!" She shouts but has her hands full. Louise ignores her.

"Jonathan, I hate to ask such a big favor, but would you take Louise upstairs and entertain her until I can get free here? Lawrence won't be a bother, but today I'm out of sorts and not willing to deal with her without swatting her bottom a good one."

"Uh, me, ma'am?" Frankly the thought of dealing with the little girl puts me off. I mean, I'm used to dealing with guys like Samuel, Georgie and those at the flop house. But a girl?

"Please, Jonathan. Juliet and I are behind schedule here, and Louise might get hurt if she stays outside much longer." During all this, Ms. Christie has yet to slow down. For a woman in her condition—most ladies by now stay hidden in their houses, not willing for the world to see them in less than perfect shape—she's not stopped living life. Nor bossing others around. I admire living life to the fullest in anyone but especially in someone carrying a real live baby.

But being a nanny... To a girl... Uh...

"Plee..aa..sse," she begs. I hate hearing the pleading voice, knowing I can do something about Louise when I can't do the chore she and Juliet are doing.

"All right, ma'am." I turn to face the wagon and child. Louise is oblivious to what's been going on behind her. "Can I toss her over my shoulder, ma'am?" I ask before my mouth can shut up the words inside. My head's come up with an idea, but I gotta get the girl upstairs first.

"As long as you don't break her, you can do whatever works," comes the unexpected answer.

Okay then. Here goes nothing.

"Miss Louise, you're coming with me. Your mama's orders." I step up behind the girl, swoop her up and toss her gentle-like over my shoulder. Swinging into an easy trot, I sing in my silly voice:

Jack and Jill went up the hill
To fetch a pail of water.
Jack fell down and broke his crown
And Jill came tumbling after.

By the time we make it into the house, Louise is giggling. "Do again," she shouts as she thumps my back in time to the rhyme. So, I sing it again in another silly sort of voice. By the time I set her down next to her brother in their nursery, she can hardly speak she's laughing so much.

"Listen, Lawrence. Jonathan is silly," she manages to get out. Lawrence with his spooky eyes cuts his glance from Louise to me, then back to the set of blocks he's stacking.

I tend to forget this pair is not quite four. I've not forgotten the feeling I get when around the boy though. Remembering my job—entertain Louise and therefore Lawrence—until Ms. Christie is finished, I break into another nursery rhyme, this time in a girl's falsetto voice. I sing and swish as if wearing a skirt. Louise rolls on the floor. Lawrence does look up from his blocks. Perhaps I have his attention as well.

Time passes without interruption. I read a story to the pair—Lawrence moves slightly closer while he listens. I pull a scarf over my head when reading the mother's part and pull on an old cap left in the nursery when reading the part of the father. Louise settles at my side with Lawrence on the other. When the girl gets too quiet, I see that she's fallen asleep.

Lawrence, though, sits like a bird with his bright eyes that see more than most others. He squirms a little. Unusual for a little one who usually sits like a statue. "Will you come again?" he asks.

I almost miss his question. I'm busy getting up without waking the little girl. Standing over him, I let my gaze meet his. Slowly, very slowly, I realize that Lawrence isn't spooky so much as he's lonely. Why doesn't he go out and play? Why doesn't he run around with his sister and brother? Why does he content himself with picture books and blocks?

My legs fold, and I squat in front of him. "You enjoyed my silliness?" He nods. "A great boy like me sounding like a creaky little lady?" He nods again. "Will you be here if I come again?" He almost nods, seems to consider the question—which I find odd—then gravely nods his head once.

I stick out my hand, making a pact with him. "Then I'll come again if you want me to."

"Yes, please."

"Done, little man." We shake solemnly.

"Now I best get back to—"

"All done, Jonathan." Ms. Christie stands in the doorway, resting her shoulder against the frame. She notes her daughter sleeping and grins. "Well done," she whispers. Noting me kneeling in front of Lawrence, she asks, "Is everything all right here?" Not worried-like. Just curious sounding.

"We're fine, Mother," Lawrence answers before I can think of anything to say. "Jonathan is fun."

"High praise indeed, Jonathan," she tells me. "Lawrence is very particular about who he chooses to like. Aren't you, dear?" She comes forward, placing a hand on my shoulder and goes to both knees in front of her son. They stretch toward each other, and she kisses his forehead as he kisses her cheek. For the oddest reason, I feel part of the love that should surround only these two.

Pushing up, still using my shoulder for support, Ms. Christie pulls me up and waves to Lawrence. "Vassy will have supper ready soon. Wash up, but don't wake your sister. Juliet will come for you both."

"Bye, Mother," the little boy says sweetly. "Bye, Jonathan. Thank you."

I can't answer even to say, 'you're welcome'. My throat is all clogged up. Must be dusty in the room...or something.

"I think you just won two hearts," Ms. Christie whispers as we descend the stairs, and she opens the back door for me to hustle back to the shop. As I thump down the back porch stairs, I swear I hear her say, "Maybe three."

———

As cold weather settles in—as cold as it ever gets here on the island, Mr. Jack and the workmen gear up for the holidays. Seems Zimmerman Furniture Factory is known for its craftsmanship, and people put in orders for holiday gifts. Seems odd to me to give furniture as a gift for Christmas, but Mr. Jack is wild with happiness over the orders flocking in. Who am I to get in a tizzy over what brings in money? What pays me each Friday?

At least I *get* paid. One of the workers broke a tool—a long-handle hand drill. I saw it break—Casper dropped it for sure, but that didn't break it. A box of wood pieces slid off a stack when he reached for the drill. Jerome, one of the other workers, actually stacked the boxes and left one at a tilt. The box fell on the handle, breaking it. An accident. I vouched for Casper to Mr. Winslow. Mr. Jack was out for the afternoon, so the accountant had the final word.

"You broke it. You pay for it," Winslow says. No matter what I said, Winslow insisted. Friday when I got my check, Casper got his—three dollars.

"How am I supposed to feed my family and pay the landlord with three dollars, Mr. Winslow?" Casper is all but crying, a great red-bearded Irishman.

"Not my concern," the accountant says and starts to close his office door in the workman's face.

"But, Mr. Winslow—"

"You will stop this now, or you'll regret it," Winslow says. His glare eats right through the man into his soul almost. Whatever Lazarus Winslow is thinking, the man knows, too. Immediately Casper clasps his mouth shut and turns away. Winslow nods like he's won an argument. Then he closes his door.

"What just happened?" I ask Thomas, a workman who's been with Mr. Jack for decades.

"Best not to ask, young man. Ol' Winslow there finds out things. And he don't mind holding them over your head."

"What's that called? Blackmail?"

"Call it what you want, youngun'. He's got Mr. Jack hornswoggled for sure. None of us gonna say nothing though. Winslow finds out things," Thomas repeats himself. He shakes his head and leaves.

"I'll be danged," I whistle under my breath. "Mr. Jack would be mad as a March Hare if he knew." I might want to settle Mr. Winslow's hash myself, but then again, I have a few secrets to keep. Best I leave well enough alone for now.

However, Casper's right. He can't buy food for his family with no more than three dollars. I got five in my paycheck. How can I help Casper without him thinking me all uppity? Whatever the plan, I need the cash first.

"Thomas, I'll be right back," I yell to the older man. He's the unofficial boss when Mr. Jack's out.

Thomas waves without looking up from the chest he's carving.

I run like greased lightning to the grocer's, and he cashes my check. But instead of putting three dollars back to me, I ask him to hold only two this time. Someone is more in need of that dollar than me.

Quick as a flash, I scoot back to the workshop. Mr. Jack's returned but has gone to the house for a few minutes. I have time to work my plan.

Casual like, I grab the push broom I use all the time and start down the aisle where Casper works. He's running a fine grit cloth over a cabinet, sanding it to a high gloss shine. While he's moving slowly, probably wondering how he's gonna tell his wife about his paycheck without telling her the reason it's short, I rustle up a pile of shavings, then

31

stop by his bench. Bending down, I pretend to pick up something. I actually have a dollar bill in my hand and run it through the shavings, so it's dusty-like.

"Hey, Casper. You drop this? I found it just now in the shavings 'neath your bench. Guess it's yours." Without giving him time to respond, I put the power on that ol' broom and shove those shavings down the aisle and out the door. Once outside, I peek around the doorframe to see what he does.

First, he feels the bill, like it's fake or something. Then he looks up and down the aisle, like someone might be watching. Finally, he smooths it off against his shirtfront and slips it into the near empty envelope that holds his puny wages for the week.

"Smart thinking, young fella," says Thomas behind me as he slips a hand on my shoulder and pats it. He must have been looking over my shoulder. "Wonder how I can slip him a bill without him thinking we're helping. It's just me and the misses at home. Not like him with a passel of kids. This week I can afford to share. I just gotta figure out how." Thomas grips my shoulder in a tight clasp, then goes off around the corner of the workshop, mumbling to himself.

———

"Man alive, it's cold," Juliet says as we haul wood in the back door of the house. We just finished filling Vassy's firebox in the kitchen of the outbuilding. "I'm plum tuckered out, but I still have to make beds in two rooms. See you later."

Juliet is a hard worker. A right pert spirit, singing now and then while she fetches and carries for Ms. Christie.

The lady is getting fleshy in the way of all ladies carrying. She's out and about though. That ain't the normal way ladies in her condition should act. She sashays up and down the street, visiting the neighbors at least once a day. "Pshaw! My way of relaxing," she tells me each time she waddles down that tall set of steps in front of the house. Now and then, I'll tote some goods for her when she visits Mrs. Mandy at the end of the block. Old lady can't hardly hear, and Ms. Christie worries that someone might break in and rob her without her even knowing someone's in the house. She's been talking to the old lady about moving into the Women's House over on Ave O 1/2. The house resembles a castle, if you ask me. A dang site better living there with other ladies than alone in a big empty house. But I reckon she has other ideas. She ain't moved yet.

Today is no day to be out visiting. But then Ms. Christie already knows that. Once again, her weather sense predicted this cold spell.

"Need any help?" I ask as Juliet sheds her coat and ties on an apron. Her long brown hair is usually in a braid but being cold, she says her hair down keeps her neck warm. Makes me warm just thinking about her... and her neck...and her hair. I'm getting hot myself, so best I skedaddle back to the workshop. It's warmer than outside but not as toasty as the front parlor.

"...besides," Juliet says as I open the back door. I must have missed whatever she said before. "I want to get Mr. Winslow's bed made before that varmint comes home."

That gets my attention. Maybe if he's flirting with Juliet that could be something I can hold over his head.

"He bothering you? Like that railroad man?"

"Naw, not like that Mr. Thrill. He's creepy."

"So, what's Winslow do?"

"Watches me. Like he don't like me. Like he thinks I might steal something of his. Gives me the willies."

"If he ever touches you, you tell me. Hear?"

"I hear. But why would I tell you?" Juliet turns saucy brown eyes my way and raises a brow just a touch.

"Well, I..." I stutter. Can't figure out how to tell her I'd flatten the man if he touched her. "Well, I... Dang it all. Just tell me." I pull my soft brim cap down over my forehead with a jerk and stomp out the door. Her laughter follows me.

"Dang women!"

———

Mr. Jack calls me into his office one day during a mild period of weather when it's warm enough to open the windows. I can smell salt carried by the breeze that comes off the gulf this time of day. Something fishy-smelling flashes past my nose now and then. Some might be afeared of being in the boss's office, but I've done nothing wrong, so I'm only curious.

"First off, Jonathan, you've worked as hard as any man around since you got here. I'm impressed. As a reward for that, you've got the day off tomorrow."

That being Saturday meant I could meet up with Georgie and Samuel. If Rowdy and Jason showed, I could avoid them.

"Thank you kindly, sir. That would be right nice. I haven't seen my friends in a week or more."

Expecting him to dismiss me, I'm surprised again when he motions me to sit in a chair next to his desk. Not the one in front of it where people sit when they come to order furniture. But the one where Ms. Christie sits when she visits.

"Jonathan," he pauses as if planning how to put whatever he wants to say. "You've become a part of my family—both here and at home. The other men approve of you, and that says a lot considering there's Irishmen, Germans and a few Italians here," he says with a soft-like chuckle.

Each man is a specialist in what he does with wood. Zimmerman's place is lucky to have each one, though they do tend to squabble over whose country is best.

"As for home, I doubt Ms. Christie can get along without you these days. You're the man she turns to when I'm not around. You run errands for her. Taste test Vassy's cooking so we don't get poisoned," he jokes. "You entertain the guests when asked and the children. Especially Lawrence. I haven't figured that out yet. But he likes you. The little fella has his problems. And he's particular as all get out. But if asked who he wants around, he says *Jonathan* without hesitation." He winks as he adds, "And you might flirt with our Juliet, but you're smart enough not to carry on with her."

A blush as hot as one of Vassy's fires runs up my body from my toes to the top of my head. "Aw, Mr. Jack," I whine in embarrassment.

He laughs and leans forward, elbows on knees, hands clasped together loose-like.

"You're a good man, Jonathan Evans. And to prove it, I'm giving you a raise."

That's the last thing I expect! A raise? Wow. Honestly, I have no words...he just blew them out of my mind.

"Cat got your tongue, youngun'?" He laughs, stands, and puts a broad hand on my shoulder. "Come on. Let's make it official. I'll tell Winslow right now to add...another dollar," he muses. "Yes, one more dollar a week to your salary. How's that, young man?" Without waiting for my reply—which isn't hard when I'm without words—he leaves the office and strides to Winslow's cubby hole.

"Lazarus, adjust the books, and show that Jonathan Evans now earns another dollar a week," he announces.

While he beams, and I stand beside him still speechless in wonder, Winslow does a slow burn. "Are you sure this is wise, sir? He's very young. Perhaps in a year or two when he's learned more about furniture making—"

"A dollar raise, if you please, Lazarus." Mr. Jack slaps Winslow on the shoulder as if the accountant agreed with the boss. The boss returns to his office, leaving me standing in Winslow's office alone.

Never one to back down from a bully, I remain quiet. Actually, I think leaving might be a good idea...follow Mr. Jack's example.

"You don't deserve this raise, you know," Winslow says quietly as he resumes his seat. He never glances my way. But I can feel the resentment rolling off him the same way Ms. Christie feels the weather changing.

I expected him to blow up over the money. The wiser thing to do with a varmint like Lazarus Winslow is to stay quiet. Without saying a word, I back out of his office. Giving him my back might rile him bad enough to do something mean. I'd be on the receiving end, and he'd be on the 'what did I do' end of the fracas.

One thing I know though: I have to watch my back all the time now.

That accountant doesn't like me. If he can get something on me, I'll have to lick his boots like the others around here.

Then again, I ain't never backed down from a challenge. Ol' Winslow might find out he's messed with the wrong fella.

———

"Georgie, you're gonna get all wet, and Sister's gonna kill you!" I yell as Georgie wades out further into water past his ankles now.

"Naw, she's not," he yells back.

"Come look. See what I got you. You won't get your clothes wet."

Curiosity brings the boy to my side. Being Saturday during early November the beach is chilly and not as crowded as summer time.

"What you got for me, Jonathan?"

"A pair of drawers and an over shirt. You can get sopping wet in these, then change when Sister shows up." I begin pulling clothes off him. He helps by wiggling, often in the opposite direction I'm pulling.

"Would you hang on there," I say in my silly squeaky voice. That gets his attention but doesn't do much for slowing him down. His clothes off— his shoes and socks hit the sand the minute Sister let him out of the wagon—I pull a cotton shirt over his head. I asked Ms. Christie if I could use an old shirt of Jackie's, and she agreed that Georgie in a swim costume would be best as the Catholic Sister might not appreciate riding home with a salty dripping young fella. She also gave me several old towels to use.

I wrap a towel around Georgie's body and tell him to drop his pants and drawers. I'd be embarrassed if someone said that to me but not this guy. He shucks out of his bottoms faster than I can get his swimming drawers ready.

"You sure it's not too cold for you, Georgie?"

"Naw, it's great!"

Of course, Georgie wouldn't tell me if he was dying of cold or not. He's having fun and not worrying about Sister fussing at him. What more can he ask for?

"Jonathan!"

Someone's calling me from down the beach a ways.

"Samuel!" My day is about perfect now. With Georgie and Samuel here, I'm with my best friends.

Samuel drops his clothes as he comes, shedding down to his own swimming suit. He shivers once but runs on and pounces on me. We wrestle in fun, careful not to go too long. Galveston folks are pretty open-minded about the Negros mixing with whites. So many folks from so many different countries are here and working and helping each other that we can't get too picky about who we hang around with. Still, no sense in riling someone on a sunny day, even if it's a tad crisp for swimming.

I roll over and sit up, Samuel beside me.

"Sure is a fine day," he says.

With nothing else to add, I just sit in silence, watching Georgie. He's prone to wading out too far.

"Days like this make it hard to believe that there's such things as bad weather," Samuel continues. "I mean, them water spouts and gulf storms and all."

"A storm wiped out Indianola back before I was born. Folks around us moved from there in order to stay safe."

"But is there really anywhere safe in this world?"

I have to think on that one. "I reckon not. But we can't live life afeared all the time."

"Not afeared maybe. Just cautious like," Samuel says. "What if life got so bad here that we had no choice but to leave. Where would you go?"

Giving him a glance—that was an odd thing to ask—my answer comes slow. "Not Houston. Too much bad stuff happens there." I don't add more. The less said about that town the better. "Maybe somewhere with lots of trees and warmth. I like this chill, but I'm not one for snow. Paw took me with him once when he got a job hauling freight to central Texas. Up by Waco. Snowed while we were there. Not a lot, but I'm not for the stuff. I like the coast. You can have those storms though."

"Not me!" Samuel says as he throws up his hands. "Last thing I want is some ol' storm rolling in, forcing me to leave this island. Only place I've ever lived. Born here," he adds proudly.

"I wasn't born here like you, but this is a pretty good place."

"We got jobs. Georgie is safe. Good people. Plenty to eat," he says that as he looks at the box sitting next to our pile of clothes.

"Ms. Vassy found out I was going to the beach. She said I might meet up with friends, so she packed me a box. There's enough food in there to feed an army."

"The three of us is an army, right?"

Laughter floods my chest. "You bet we are! Hey, Georgie! Come eat!"

Good friends. Good food. Good day for the beach. What more can a person ask for indeed!

I suppose the smile on Sister's face and a friendly nod to Samuel and me as she drives away with a dry Georgie is something special.

Being invited to spend the night with Samuel and his family is really special, too. He's got a big family; I've spent time with them before. His maw is from the Carrib and knows about fancy cooking. My mouth waters as he and I dress, covered with Ms. Christie's towels, then heap towels and trash into Vassy's box—that's now empty—and trudge down the beach toward the east end of the island.

Letting Mrs. Abbey know I'll not be at the flop house that night or letting Mr. Jack and Ms. Christie know I'll be with a friend never enters my mind.

TURNING POINT

Sunday morning doesn't dawn so much as happens. Fog so thick you can cut it settles over the island. An icy fog too. I didn't take my jacket to the beach yesterday, so I'm gonna walk half way across the island to the Zimmerman's boarding house using only a towel or two to ward off the chill. I'll return Miss Vassy's box, then head over to Mrs. Abbey's house.

I swear the fog is an odd one. Sounds fall flat. The wet stuff almost feels evil, wrapping itself around your legs as you walk. Samuel and his sisters duck back inside to the fireplace almost as soon as I clear the steps. Not having a buggy, Mr. Perkins can't offer me a ride up town. If I didn't know the way, I'd be lost in no time. Glad that Samuel and his family only have to go to the Negro church and back and glad that Georgie is safe at St. Mary's, I plod along. Now and then, a church song filters through the fog when I'm near such a place. Getting to Avenue L that day is about the longest walk I can remember ever taking.

Best I leave Ms. Vassy's food box at the kitchen door, I think, as I near the Zimmerman's place. The towels I'll hang over the back porch railing. Then I'll hoof it over to Mrs. Abbey's house and change clothes. Samuel's maw was kind enough to let me wash up there. Guess she didn't want to have me stinking up the place. 'Course Samuel was right there alongside me with a rag and hot water. He laughed at me when Mrs. Perkins handed me that rag and a bit of soap, then the laugh was my turn when she did the same to her son. Nice lady even if she's not one for salty boys at her table.

Fog fills the tiny back yard of the boarding house. If I didn't know where the kitchen steps are, I'd probably break my neck finding them. I figure Vassy's inside setting the table for breakfast. All the boarders are in for the weekend. Winslow, of course, as well as the railroad men, McGraw and that nasty ol' Thrill who come and go. Mr. Newmann who works at the newspaper. He's a typesetter, the guy who puts all the letters in order for the stories the reporters bring in. The boarding house is his home, like Winslow. Same for Mr. Fuller who owns a hardware store and Mr. Jones who supervises loading on the docks. A full house, Ms. Christie says most days.

Rather than bother them, I tiptoe across the yard, aware that no one can really see me for the dense fog. It's gotten thicker. I feel for the railing along the steps and touch something alive.

A face comes closer, then a scream loud enough to bust my ears vibrates through the fog! Dang it all! Who? Juliet? Quick as a wink I drop the towels in time to catch her as she faints dead away! What the hell's going on here?

Feet pound down the hall. The back door opens and another scream! Who?

"Miss Vassy?" Mr. Fuller shouts. He's a kind man, probably taking care of the cook.

I'm holding Juliet across my lap and hear a thud. Someone else fainted?

"For God's sake, someone help," Fuller pleads.

"Who's there?" comes Mr. Jack's voice.

"It's just me...Jonathan. Why'd she do this?" I ain't never had a woman fall into my lap.

"Jonathan?" Footsteps rush down the stairs, and a hand reaches out to me. Hands trace my face. Another face gets so close to mine that our noses almost touch. "Jonathan!" Mr. Jack looms up so close I feel suffocated. I swear he looks like he might pass away like the ladies!

Arms hug me so tight I'm afeared I'll drop Juliet who's coming out of her faint.

"Whath gog oonn?" I'm trying to get answers here, but first Mr. Jack, then Juliet, then Ms. Christie are hugging me and crying over me. Vassy can't get to me, but I can hear her crying and praying at the same time. I'm about strangled with all this attention. I gotta have air.

Arms move away as I struggle to take a deep breath and make sense of all this strange behavior.

"Oh, Jonathan," Ms. Christie says as she manages to sit on the step next to me. "We thought..." She breaks down and cries.

Now I'm scared.

"What's going on?" I demand, fear making my voice sharper than I intend. Juliet sits at my feet, holding my hand, tears streaming down her face as well.

"Son, we got word from the police early this morning that you were..."

Even Mr. Jack is choked up?

"What, sir? That I was what?"

"Dead."

Say what? Dead, they say? How can I be dead?

"Not by a jugful, sir." I thump my chest to show him I'm breathing. I'm scared, but more than that, I can't figure out what's going on.

All this carrying on is getting to me. "Come on, Juliet...Ms. Vassy. Stop crying, please. You're giving Ms. Christie fits."

I pat Ms. Christie's hand where it clutches my arm. "Ma'am, you gotta stop this caterwaulin'. Ain't good for you or the baby. I'm all right." I stand, pull Juliet up beside me, then reach down for Mr. Jack's hand. "Help me get her up, sir. She needs to be outta this fog. Dang stuff's thick as soup."

We manage to get each other up and inside, moving through the boarders who stand gawking like turkeys in the rain. One odd thing I notice as we sit Ms. Christie at the table is Mr. Winslow. The man looks like he's seen a ghost. And he ain't looking happy about my resurrection apparently.

"Jonathan," Ms. Christie starts, but her words drown in tears that still race down her cheeks. She alternates between clasping both hands over her face and wringing them in the edge of her apron.

"Son, we thought you were dead. The police came just before dawn to say the house where you and the other boys live burned down."

"Burned? Mrs. Abbey? Is she—?"

"The lady who owns the house—Mrs. Abbey?—is fine. Two of your friends got her out before the house collapsed. But..." He stopped and swallowed. "The firemen found a body in the room where you sleep."

Jesus! That wasn't me. I was at Samuel's house. Who died in that fire? Why do they think it was me?

"Why me? I wasn't even there last night. I spent the night with that Negro boy, Samuel. You remember him? You met him on the beach. He's been around a few times."

"Mrs. Abbey said you came in last night." Mr. Jack sounded as confused as me.

"Oh, well, that explains it. She gets me mixed up with Willie all the time. We look a lot alike. He must have come in, gone to bed and..." The idea of dying in a fiery bed makes me sick to my stomach.

"You all right, son?" Mr. Jack holds me up as I lean toward the floor.

Suddenly his steady hand ain't enough. I make a dash for the back door and the porch rail. The bread and sausage Mrs. Perkins fed us this morning hurls out over the oleander bushes.

"Come inside, Jonathan." Mr. Jack steadies me as I wobble back to the table.

"Sorry, ma'am." Ms. Christie looks worn out, almost as sick as me. I don't want to add more troubles to what they thought they had before I showed up.

"Better to be sick in the flowers than be dead," Ms. Christie says, her hand reaching out for mine. I hold it in a grip that's sure to hurt but, at the moment, I need to feel something alive. The memory of her big belly pressed against me out on the porch is comforting in a strange way.

"Anyone else hurt, sir?" I gotta know if Rowdy and Jason were in the room. I might not like them too much at times, but they've been good to me.

"No one else, the police think."

"Oh, my God!" Ms. Christie exclaims.

"You all right, ma'am?" I jump up, scared she's gonna have that baby right here and now.

"Fine, Jonathan. Fine..." She pats my hand, then takes it to hold on to again. "We have to let the police know that the boy who died isn't our Jonathan." She turns confused eyes to me. "You think he was this Willie?"

"Probably, ma'am. Mrs. Abbey is a kind ol' lady but gets a bit muddled when it comes to which of us is which. We look enough alike to be... Well, like twins."

At that moment, the Zimmerman children barrel down the staircase, much to their mother's disgrace, I'm sure—Lawrence moving slower than his sister and brother. They hurl themselves into my arms.

"We thought something happened to you. Mama was crying, and Papa paced the floor, his face all scrunched up," Jackie says as he screws up his face, trying to show how Mr. Jack must have looked.

"I'm fine, younguns'. Fine. Now let me breathe." Jackie and Louise step back but only a small step. Lawrence, however, still clings to me, his arms around my waist, his face buried in my shirtfront.

"It'll be fine, little man. I'm here now," I whisper low. A few pats on the shoulder and he, too, steps back. But tears streak his face just like his maw's.

"Jonathan, you and I will take the buggy to Mrs. Abbey's house and speak to the police, then find your landlady and let her know you're not dead. That might not make her feel any better, to know she confused two boys. But it's the right thing to do."

A thought hits me, sudden like.

"Mr. Jack, can we drive to the orphanage—to St. Mary's—and see Georgie?"

"That little boy? Your best friend?"

"Yes, sir. Samuel might hear, but he'll know I'm okay 'cause I spent the night at his house. But if Georgie hears and doesn't know better, then..." The thought chokes me up, so I can't finish.

"Of course, we can go there, and let him know that you're all right... just in case he hears anything to the contrary," Mr. Jack agrees.

He pauses to look over the group in the dining room. Ms. Christie still sits at the end of the table, her face all blotchy from crying. Juliet stands as close to me as possible and looks pretty much the same way. Only she's holding her apron in both hands, wringing the ends and occasionally using them to dry more tears. Vassy has disappeared. I no sooner notice that than she comes through the swinging doors, carrying a coffee pot. She gives me a nod, indicating the cups on the sideboard.

"Here, ma'am," I hold up a cup and saucer, so Vassy can pour the dark liquid safely. "Sip this, then eat a bit." I hate to pull Mr. Jack away, while she might still need him, but I want to get over to Mrs. Abbey's place. Or what's left of it. Then go see Georgie.

I turn pleading eyes on Mr. Jack, hoping he'll understand how anxious I am.

"Darling, Jonathan and I have a few things to do. We'll return in time for supper. Maybe before dinner. Perhaps instead of going to church this morning you might have a lay-down instead? Vassy and Juliet can handle things until we return." He urges her up and motions for Juliet to bring the coffee. "Children, go up to the nursery, and stay quiet while Mother rests." While mild, his tone brooks no argument. His gentle hands guide his wife and children toward the staircase. His nod to Vassy and Juliet send them up as well.

"You gentlemen may serve yourselves this morning, I'm sure," Mr. Jack tells the boarders gathered round.

My legs grow weak, and I sit heavily in the chair Ms. Christie just abandoned. Mr. Fuller offers me a cup of coffee, but the thought of eating makes my stomach turn again. I swallow bile and shake my head. He lays the cup aside and motions the other men to the table.

Sunk in misery, I pay no attention to the boarders, most of whom are filling their cups with coffee. Out of the corner of my eye, I catch sight of Lazarus Winslow, staring hard at me.

"Boy, how is it you weren't at home last night?"

"I met friends yesterday, and one of them invited me to his house for the night." I've already said that, but maybe he wasn't near enough to hear.

Thankfully, he makes no response. I'm not in the mood to play his games today.

Mr. Jack comes down the stairs, pulls his jacket off the hall tree, then pulls another off as well. He hands the second one to me, while he pulls on the first. "Ready?"

"Yes, sir." Without a backwards glance, we set off to right a wrong.

———

"Willie? Nooo! Jonathan!" Mrs. Abbey runs to me, as wobbly as she is, and hugs me until once again I'm afeared I'll be strangled. I pat her awkwardly on the back. Two policemen in uniforms, Mr. Jack, a detective in a suit and two firemen stand around watching. Embarrassed at having yet another crying woman hanging on my neck, I ease Mrs. Abbey away at least an arm's length.

"Yes, ma'am. It's me. That other fella..." I can't finish the sentence. After all, she led the authorities to think the dead boy was me. Wasn't her fault, but still she'll feel guilty. I know the old lady. She'd never intentionally hurt anyone on purpose.

An older couple stand nearby as well. Seems they took Mrs. Abbey into their home a few houses down the street after the firemen said her house wasn't safe to stay in. They step forward now and take her by the arms, gentle-like. She walks away with them but waves goodbye to me. "I'm so glad you're safe, dear."

Once she's gone, I turn to gander at the place where I used to live. What a mess. The back section of the house with the two bedrooms Mrs. Abbey rented out are nothing but burned boards tumbled onto soggy ground. Seems the fire department showed up after all. But they saved nothing here. Oh, maybe they saved the houses tightly packed on either side, but Mrs. Abbey's home is gone. The few things I had are gone. Seems my life is once again taking a drastic turn.

I wander over to stand beside Mr. Jack who introduces me to the detective—a man named Mortimer.

"Son, you're a lucky one. That fella that died didn't die in the fire though."

"What?" Both Mr. Jack and I say at the same time.

"We examined the body and discovered his head was bashed in. Most likely the boy was dead before the fire began. After checking the area, the firemen and I think this may have been arson. Perhaps the fire was set to hide the fact the boy was murdered."

"Murdered!" If Willie's death was a sad enough affair, then his murder puts things in a different light.

"Mrs. Abbey said she didn't think Willie—let's see, his name is Willie Sanders—had any relatives. That true?"

"Yes, sir. He told me, Rowdy and Jason once that his folks died in that last influenza bout, and he was on his own." A thought hits me. "What about the other fellas that stayed here? Four usually sleep in the other room. There's me, Rowdy and Jason. What about them?"

"All the others have been accounted for. Only the Sanders boy died. You have any idea why someone would kill the kid?"

"Me? I barely knew him. Didn't cotton to some of the things he said he did in order to live. We just shared a room, that's all."

"Okay," the detective says as he folds up his small notebook and tucks it into his pocket. "Where will you be staying in case we need to talk to you again?"

"I uh... I uh..." Where *will* I stay? I have no home...or at least no place to sleep each night. I can't stay with Samuel. Too many in his family as is. And too far to walk back and forth to the Zimmerman's place for work. "I uh...don't know—" I begin, but Mr. Jack cuts in.

"He'll be at my place—Zimmerman's boarding house on Avenue L and Tremont. I'm Jack Zimmerman. My wife and I own the boarding house, and I run Zimmerman's Furniture workshop."

"Yes, sir. I've heard of you. My wife bought one of your small chests a few years back," the detective says with a grin. "Take care of the lad. We don't know if this was a case of mistaken identity and Jonathan here was the intended victim or whether Willie Sanders was the target. Either way, be safe." He tips his hat to Mr. Jack and leaves us.

"Can you imagine?" Mr. Jack says as he turns once again to stare at the burned home. "I'm sorry for your friend, Willie."

"He was more a fella that showed up each night, sir. Not really a friend. But to die with a bashed-in head, then be burned up..." I gulp once more. My imagination runs wild. I need to rein it in, or I'll never sleep again.

"Come on, young fella. Let's go find your friend, Georgie." Mr. Jack leads me to the buggy, and off we head down the island, out along the beach a good three miles to St. Mary's Orphan Asylum.

———

"Excuse me, Sister, but we're looking for a boy named Georgie." Mr. Jack stands, hat in hand, with me in the front hall of the orphanage. Silence feels real on the inside. Outside the sound of children comes to me. Bet Georgie's not inside.

"Let me check. Wait here, please." A nun—what the Catholics call a sister—glides away, silent in habit as well as motion.

We wait for a good five minutes before anyone shows up.

A different sister comes this time. "I believe you'll find George outside with the animals." The sister leads us to the front steps and points in the direction of a barn. Then like her sister nun, she folds her hands inside the long sleeves of her gown and walks away.

Mr. Jack and I exchange shrugs and head to the barn. We pass other children, much younger than Georgie, but just as energetic if their game of chase is any proof.

"Jonathan!" Georgie must have caught sight of us before we got too near the place. He bounds out, sees Mr. Jack and slows to a slight run rather than the jubilant gallop he started with.

"Hey ya, Georgie," I say when he comes near enough for me to hug. "How you doing, fella?"

"Fine, but Jonathan, why are you out here?" He's asking me the question but eyeing Mr. Jack at the same time.

"You remember Mr. Jack...right? From the beach? I work for him."

"Yes. Hello, sir." Georgie reaches out and shakes Mr. Jack's hand like an adult. I'm real proud to see he has some manners.

"Georgie, is there a place where we can sit and talk private-like?" I ask, looking around at what appears to be a yard of youngsters.

"Sure, come into the barn. I just stacked some hay bales. We can sit there." He dashes off, remembers us, then slows and motions toward the right side of the barn's interior. Sure enough, several bales of hay make a perfect sitting place.

"Georgie, remember Mrs. Abbey?"

"Sure, she gave me some cookies last time I went to your house."

"Do you ever remember meeting a fella named Willie?"

"No, but you told me Mrs. Abbey always gets you and him mixed up 'cause you look so much alike. Why? What's wrong?"

Mr. Jack said he'd let me tell Georgie the story, but it's hard to find a way to start.

"Uh, Georgie, after you left the beach yesterday, I stayed the night with Samuel—"

"Ah, that's not fair, Jonathan! You know I like going to his house," Georgie whines.

"Georgie, will you just shut up for a minute, and listen to me."

"Uh, all right, Jonathan. I'll be quiet." True to his word, a stunned Georgie clamps his lips tightly shut.

If anyone can look like they been pole-axed upside the head, it's this fella. I don't usually get bossy with the little man. I let out a huff of air, wipe the nervous sweat off my upper lip and try again.

"Last night, Mrs. Abbey's house burned down, and Willie didn't make it out of the fire." I rush to say the words without giving him any of the murder/arson details. He's too young for all that.

"Gee whiz, Jonathan! What about the other fellas—Rowdy and Jason?" Georgie sits there, his mouth hanging open like a beached fish.

"Haven't seen them, but they made it out of the fire, the police said. Only one person died, and that's Willie."

"But you're all right...right, Jonathan?" Georgie's eyes are tearing up. He scoots over to my hay bale and presses close to my side, like Lawrence does sometimes.

"Right as rain, little man," I assure him with an arm over his shoulders. "I just didn't want you to ride into town and hear about a fire—and such—thinking it was me that died."

Georgie has nothing to say to that.

"Listen, Mr. Jack and I have a long way to go to get back to town. You'll be okay here?" I pull Georgie around, so I can see his face. For as long as I've known him, his face tells me if he's lying.

He nods, perhaps too anxious to speak. But at the last second, he answers in a tiny voice, "I'll be all right, Jonathan."

"There you are, gov!" I hug him tight for a second as I talk in my silly voice. "We're off! See ya soon, mate!"

"Thanks, Jonathan," Georgie whispers. He nods to Mr. Jack, stands and a heartbeat before he dashes out of the barn, he jumps up atop a hay bale and swats me along the back of the head.

Mr. Jack laughs as we make our way to the buggy, while I rub the sore spot the little man left behind.

———

"Let's find Ms. Christie and see if Vassy can rustle up some hot tea. I'm about froze through," Mr. Jack says as we leave the barn that's well beyond the back of the house and kitchen out-building. Old Gerty seemed more than ready to return to her warm stall and a bucket of oats and a long drink of clean water.

My stomach growls about the time we swing into the kitchen.

"Vassy!"

She pops up on the other side of the long counter that runs down the center of the kitchen. "Right here, Mr. Jack. Just pulling out some bowls to use. Buried they were in the bottom cabinet." She places two large bowls on the counter, then uses her apron to dust of her hands.

"Jonathan and I are about froze from that long buggy ride. The fog's still hanging on. I'll be glad when the sun comes out. Dreary today." He's almost rambling. I poke him with my elbow but gentle-like. He's an adult and my boss after all. Still, food sounds pretty good right about now. The smells in the kitchen alone make my stomach growl again.

"Oh yeah, right. Vassy, do you think you might prepare some tea for us and maybe some sandwiches or cookies or muffins…or something. We're cold, starved and thirsty."

"I think I can handle that. You'll be in the Missus' room?"

"That we will." He turns but remembers his manners. "Thank you, Vassy, for helping Ms. Christie this morning."

"I ain't done a thing to help," she protests.

"Ah, but you kept the boarders happy with your fine food and too distracted to bother my wife with silly question she had no answer for. For that," he bows crisply, "I thank you."

"Aw, Mr. Jack, get on with you." Her slight German accent comes out with her embarrassment, but she's all smiles as we leave the kitchen and bound up the back steps.

"Come along, Jonathan. Ms. Christie will want to see you and hear how it went at the house and with Georgie." I'm not wild about barging in on the lady. But Mr. Jack pulls my jacket sleeve so off I go.

Being the middle of a Sunday afternoon, the house is quiet. I hear someone in the parlor turn the pages of a newspaper. A low murmur from the checker table corner tells me two are playing the game. There's no noise from the children.

Mr. Jack notices that, too. "The children must be in our room with their mother." He adds quietly, "Or they're taking a nap."

The closer I get, the more I want to turn back. I'm not feeling so good about traipsing into Mr. Jack's bedroom. Even the family room upstairs. It's for…well, family. Best I cut out now and try to figure out where to stay the night from now on.

"Uh, Mr. Jack?" I catch his arm as he heads down the hall, expecting me to follow, I'm sure.

"Yes?"

"Ain't right for me to be up here with the family. I'm just hired help. I thank you for your help today. With the police and Georgie. But I better get back to...to..." I stop like hitting a wall. Where will I *get back to*?

Mr. Jack stops, turns to face me and studies me for a few seconds. He winks and says, "I think I understand how you feel, but, son, you're in need of some advice and maybe a bed. Besides, Ms. Christie will ask about you first thing when I show up. If you're not there to answer her questions, she'll just send me to find you. So, might as well come in now as later."

I hesitate. "I don't know—"

"Trust me. She wants to see you as much as she wants to see me," he assures me as he puts a hand behind me and guides me to the door.

"Yes, sir. If you say so," I mutter as he guides me through.

"I do."

We pass into the family room. Sure enough, Jackie, Louise and Lawrence sit on the floor. Louise has an art pad and colors. Lawrence is looking at a picture book, and Jackie studies a magazine about fishing. They jump up when they see their father.

"Papa!"

"Shhh!" he whispers. Immediately the three speak quieter though they hug his neck. Amazing how big a hug can be—he's got all three inside his arms.

"Is everything all right, Papa?" Lawrence asks. Jackie and Louise seem content with their paw being back. Lawrence is the one with the questions.

"Things are fine, son." Lawrence gets an extra hug.

"Jonathan, are you all right?"

Emotions don't come quick to me, but the little fella's concern gets to me right away. "Right as rain, little man," I give him as I lean down to his level and wink.

Something in the way Lawrence stands relaxes. I can see tension leave his shoulders and face. He now appears as content to have his family back as his sister and brother.

"Is Mama asleep?" Mr. Jack asks the little boy.

"No, sir. She's sitting at the window, just watching the fog roll down the block."

"Thank you, son. Now go back to your book and let Jonathan and me talk to your mama."

Lawrence joins his sister and brother, and we continue to the bedroom door.

If I could blush, I would. I mean, going into a private bedroom. But Mr. Jack all but pulls me inside, so I have no choice without looking like we're fighting. My muscles tense up though, and I have the darnedest temptation to turn and run. Where to, I have no idea, but running sounds good.

Except for a tall bed tucked into the far side of the room, the place is rather pretty. Not fussy like Mrs. Abbey's house...like it used to be. Tall chests probably hold clothes. An armoire holds dresses. All those are on the far side with the bed. If you look toward the other side of the room, the side with the big window, facing the front of the house, it's like seeing an entirely different place. To one side is a small roll top desk. That must be Mr. Jack's because across from it on the other side of the large window is a small writing table with a high back that has cubby holes for paper and all the things ladies like to use. My maw wanted one of those little desks. Paw said the cost was too dear. She never got one, but that didn't stop her from wishing for one.

Between the two desks sit two deep cushioned chairs. The kind that you sit in, put your feet up on to a little padded stool and doze off for a nap. Between those stands a carved wooden table—like the ones I see in Mr. Jack's furniture workshop. He must have made that for her.

The remains of a muffin or cake cover a small plate. Beside that is an empty cup, set in a delicate saucer.

Ms. Christie sits with her back to us, staring out the window. In her lap, or what's left of it, she holds a Bible.

"My dear?" Mr. Jack whispers. To avoid scaring her, I'm sure. She looks lost in thought.

"Jack?" She turns, hard as that probably is, sees him and holds out her arms. Her hug is as hardy as the one Mr. Jack gave the children. "And Jonathan?" She looks over his shoulder and spots me standing quietly by the door. "Come here, you dear boy," she invites.

Jack helps her stand, and she moves toward me. I take a step or two toward her, not sure what to do next. But Ms. Christie knows. She hugs me so hard I'm afeared she'll strangle me again. This time though, she lets go quick-like.

"You all right?" she asks as she brushes hair off my forehead. Just like Maw used to do.

"Yes, ma'am."

She wraps her arm through mine, using it for support as she pulls me back toward the chairs and table. "I'm glad. It's been a hard day for you... losing your friend and a place to live at the same time."

Mr. Jack waits until she sits before he pulls a chair from his desk and places it between them at the table. "Take a seat, Jonathan. Vassy should be here soon."

Me? At a table with them? Ain't right!

That man must read my mind like Samuel does now and then. He all but drags me into the chair. "Sit," he commands but winks to show he's not mad.

Knuckes rap on the door, and he calls out, "Enter."

Juliet opens the door, but Vassy enters carrying a full tray. Mr. Jack immediately hops up and takes it from her. "This is heavy, Vassy. You brought a ton of food." He isn't complaining by any means. He practically drools over the selection she's brought. He places the tray on the table, and I begin drooling.

A deep belly laugh escapes Ms. Christie. "You two look like dogs before food bowls. Go on. Pour their tea, Vassy, while I make plates for them."

We sit like kings, while the ladies pour hot tea with sugar and set the cup and saucers down beside plates loaded with small sandwiches, cookies and a muffin as big as my fist. The day's been a long one, and I'm hungry, but I'm not about to touch anything until Mr. or Mrs. Zimmerman do.

Ms. Christie sits back in her chair, closes her eyes and whispers, "Lord, thank you for this day. For the safety of our dear Jonathan. For this food that I'm sure they want to eat right now." She eases one eye open as if checking to see that we're not cheating and snitching a bit. With a nod that we're both waiting, she finishes. "Help us do good and remember You in all ways. Amen."

"All right, gentlemen. I think you'd best eat before your tea gets cold."

Neither Mr. Jack nor I need a second invitation.

Sometime later, I flop back in the chair and rub my stomach. I never realized how hungry I was until I started on that plate of food. And the tea...I've never been one for tea except when I'm sick—Maw used to dose me with hot tea and honey when my throat hurt. But this tea is hot and sweet. After that windy buggy ride through spooky fog banks thick enough to make me wonder where the path was, I admit tea suits me just fine.

Given the warmth of the room thanks to a fire in the fireplace, I'm about as content as a man could get. Now if I could just figure out where to bed down tonight.

Ms. Christie sets her teacup down and turns her attention back to the window. Beyond the glass, fog swirls. The white world blocks sight of tall old homes with palms, oleanders, and a huge cottonwood tree I know rises above the house across the street. Yards filled with roses, day lilies and lantana like Maw used to have are invisible. What I'd give to see the sun right now.

With the dreary day, yesterday's memories of the beach disappear when I remember Willie died in a fire on the one night I wasn't there.

"Jonathan?" Mr. Jack pulls my attention away from the window. Out of the corner of my eye, I see Ms. Christie straighten, though she still focuses on the window. Is she listening to us or thinking something else?

"Yes, sir?"

"Where will you live now?"

"Uh, I'm not real sure, sir. I mean, I have a little money saved—the green grocery holds onto it for me. I guess I can go scout out a place to live in, but Mrs. Abbey was nice to me, and we didn't have so many boys in one room that it was a mess." I shrug, clearly at a loss. "Honestly? I have no dang idea where I'll go when I leave here today."

"Jonathan," Mr. Jack begins. He leans forward in his chair, one with a tall back and curved sides that protects against drafts and gives you a nice place to lay your head. I've never sat in a chair like that, but there's one in the parlor. Mr. Jones falls asleep in it now and then after his shift at the docks. I catch him there when I bring things over to Ms. Christie. He usually works nights. Guess he finds the chair more comfortable than his bed, but I can't see how.

"What would you say if we..." He points to himself and his wife. "... ask you to stay here? Live with us. You're a fine young man. You're easy to be around, and you hold your temper well. I've seen that at the workshop."

"But sir, you don't know me! You don't know a thing about me," I protest. What I say is true. There are secrets I hold. One not bad at all, but the Zimmermans might get upset if they found out. The other one? A bad seed is what I might be. I don't want to be near Ms. Christie and her kids if that comes true. Mr. Jack wouldn't like my secret. Ms. Christie would cry maybe, but she'd be pulling Jackie, Louise, Lawrence, and this new baby away from me as she did—denying me the pleasure of their company. "I'm not such a good person maybe," I whisper as I hang my head.

"Jonathan, have you killed anyone?"

"What? No, sir!" What a question to ask. I gulp though. It hits close to home.

"Have you stolen from anyone?"

"No, sir. Not once even when I was hungry."

"Have you ever lied?"

Oh Lord, that he asks that question. I put off my answer as long as possible but finally admit, "Maybe."

"Did the lie hurt someone?"

55

Now that one I have to think about. The first lie is an innocent one meant to protect someone. That's not a hurtful lie. The second one…well, maybe that's not so hurtful either. I mean, the only-est one that might get hurt would be me. Guess I'm protecting myself from hurt. Wonder if I can answer so Mr. Jack—and Ms. Christie 'cause I know she's listening—will understand.

"Any lie I've said would only hurt me, sir, if someone found out," I admit.

"I can't ask you to never lie to us, Jonathan. That's almost against human nature. But would you try to be as honest with us as possible?"

"But, Mr. Jack, I'm just a common fella. I smoke—now and then. I cuss—now and then. I like spending time on the beach after work instead of being all social-like with the boarders. What if I do something wrong?" A hundred things go through my mind—ninety-nine of them awful damaging things to the idea of living here. The last of that one hundred, though, is a tiny thing called hope.

Mr. Jack laughs. "You're not a saint, Jonathan! No one expects you to be one," he adds quieter. "Would you ever do anything to hurt the children?"

"No, sir!" I answer indignantly.

"What about Ms. Christie?"

On that one, I jump up fast. "Now you're just being mean, Mr. Jack. I ain't never had cause to hurt anyone here and don't plan on having cause." Mad as a hornet, I stomp toward the door.

"Jonathan." She calls my name so softly I almost don't hear above the thud of my boots on the floorboards.

But that tiny woman with the big belly grabbed my heart long ago, and I can't ignore her.

"Yes, ma'am?"

"Would you let me use your arm to keep me steady as we stroll around the house? Out the back door, I think, around the outside of the fence, along the side of the street, then up the front steps. Not far. I don't think I can walk that far, but I want to feel the day."

I know the route she wants to take. Not a long walk at all. I know the reason. She wants to taste the fog, feel it, listen to the sounds. Sense the weather. What I don't know is why she wants *me* to go with her.

I hesitate, not because I don't want to help her, but because I know she can knock down everything I just said. My being in this house will never hurt anyone, if I can help it. If moving in even happens.

Mr. Jack sits back in his chair, a smile on his lips and one brow raised a little. Like a checker player who's backed the other player into a corner and is just waiting for the fella to admit defeat.

"Jonathan?"

"Yes, ma'am. I'll walk with you. You might want to put on a coat, ma'am. I'll get my jacket and meet you downstairs. That work?"

"That would work perfectly, sir. I'll be there directly. Shall we meet at the back door or on the back porch?" She turns to look at me around the edge of that chair's high side.

I sigh and give up. She's got me. "On the back porch, ma'am."

"Gonna grab one of those smokes?"

Before I can answer...the woman can read minds, too...she adds, "Don't smoke in the house or around the children, please."

"Yes, ma'am. Meet you on the porch." Defeated, I trudge downstairs, seeing the house in a new way this time. Without a word to anyone, I snatch my jacket off the hall tree and plop my flat cap on my head. Giving the little bill a decided jerk down in order to hide my eyes as best I can, I head to the porch. Immediately I pull out my last smoke and two fire sticks. In the dampness swirling tightly in the small back yard, the first stick goes out right off. The last one finally gets the smoke lit.

Several deep draws bring a bit of calm to my nerves. No one's ever asked me to live with them. I think of Georgie. Wonder what he'd say to this? Wonder if Samuel can even imagine this? Like as not, that black boy would say, "I told you so".

I pull the last puff out of the smoke just as the back screen opens. Ms. Christie holds it, so it won't bang shut—something Jackie does all the time. Not letting the door shut easy but letting it bang as he runs down the steps.

"Ready?"

I'm not ready for this one little bit but putting off Ms. Christie is like holding back a gulf storm...just not happening.

"Yes, ma'am." I throw down the smoke and use the toe of my boot to scrunch it out. No sense letting another house go up in flames. "Best move over to the edge, so you can hold on while we go down. This fog's got the steps all slippery."

"Right. Your arm please, sir."

She calls me *sir* at times, like I'm a grown-up. Makes my chest feel funny...all puffed up a bit.

Together we make our way down the steps that are indeed so damp it's like being in the rain without the rain. Ms. Christie walks slowly, due to her size. No one's ever said when this baby is due, but I can't help notice that the bulk no longer sits up high under her chest but low, like in her lap. But then again, I've only seen one lady about to have a baby. I remember Maw looked like this not long before she birthed that little girl.

In silence, we make our way across the yard. At the picket gate, she stops and leans for a moment. I'd say she's tired, but I recognize that look now. She's listening to the weather, the fog, the breeze too slight to brush away this soupy mess. She holds out a hand and watches the whiteness swirl around each finger like a piece of ribbon.

A shiver passes down my back. I'd say this is too spooky for me, but this is me and Ms. Christie. Nothing spooky about it. I do admit it's odd though, watching her play with that stuff.

"Come, Jonathan. Let me see what's going on." We step out onto the wooden sidewalk that runs down beside the fence. Barely wide enough for us both, I walk next to the street in case someone comes barreling along in a buggy and doesn't see us.

Even with that far-off look on her face, she pats my arm. "Thank you for helping me. I needed some fresh air. The sunshine will be so nice when it comes out Tuesday."

Tuesday? "You mean we have to go through another day of this stuff?" I can't help but be dismayed. Nothing more depressing to the spirit than fog.

"Afraid so. The sun will be lovely, but sadly this fog will be with us a bit longer."

We go along, our footstep invisible in the sounds of the fog. My steps are closer, so I can walk at her pace instead of my usual wide-open stride. I have yet to see the end of the fence that signals us turning right to go up to the front gate. Are we really going that slow?

Just when I think we can make it back into the house and I can avoid answering Mr. Jack's question about moving in with them, Ms. Christie brings it right out in the open.

"You will stay, won't you?"

"But—"

"Why 'but'?" she wants to know.

"All those things I told Mr. Jack—that you heard. I ain't a nice person at times. I've lived a hard life for years now. Roughing around. Some of my friends aren't the kind you want around the children."

"Then only ask those friends here that you know won't hurt them," she challenges.

"Well, ma'am, that would only leave Georgie and Samuel. And lots of white folks don't let Negroes come into their houses."

"True, but by now you know we're not that kind of white folks," she says as innocent as a babe.

"What will your boarders say if I move in?" I can feel my resistance crumbling like a week-old cookie. "What're they gonna say if Samuel comes over?"

"Well, Jonathan, I suppose those mean-spirited bodies will just have to find another place to live."

I stop—struck dumb with shock—so she has to stop as well.

She laughs when she sees me, staring all open-mouthed and goggle-eyed.

"Surprised?"

"Ms. Christie, you can't do that!"

"Why not?" Again, with that innocent look that I know she's faking.

"I'm nobody! You can't turn your house upside down for me!"

"You don't think highly of yourself, sir." She throws at me as she pulls my arm to get us going again.

"I have no reason to think any higher of myself than I am right now. I'm poor and a nobody. Hell, I don't even have a clean shirt or pants to my name," I say, wanting to yell at this hardheaded woman.

She stops us this time. She turns to face me and puts both hands on her waist, wide as it is right now. "You listen to me, Jonathan Evans. Mr. Jack and I admire and like you enough to trust our home and family to you. We want you to live with us." She gives her head such a sharp nod, she almost topples forward. "Enough of this self-doubt, fussing and fuming. You'll live here and like it!" she shouts.

"But—" I say, holding out my hands, trying to get her to see my side of things.

"No more buts, young man!" She stomps her foot but almost loses her balance.

Quick as a wink I grab her arm. "Ma'am, you need to get inside and sit down." I wrap her hand around my arm again. "Right now, and no arguing." I try to move her forward, but she won't budge. "Come on, Ms. Christie," I plead.

"Only if you say yes," she demands and sticks her nose in the air like some prim missy.

"For the love of God, will you come on or not?" I can see us turning into statues out here. Dang woman is stubborn as a mule!

"Jonathan, say yes..." She won't look at me for the longest, but then she does, cuts those green eyes my way and raises her chin. "...or here I stand."

"Yes! Yes! Now will you get moving? This fog has turned your brain to mush!" I grumble as she starts moving again. "About time you get a move on."

"Don't fuss, sir. It isn't polite to fuss at a lady in my condition," she points out with a sharp nod of her head, all serious-like, despite the fact she just yelled at me.

But I see a tiny smile lift the edges of her lips. She won this argument. Why did I ever think I had a chance against her?

I snort but manage to get her through the gate and started up the steps. Mr. Jack magically appears and holds out a hand for his wife. "How goes it, my dear?"

"The weather is foul and will stay so for a day or so more, but our Jonathan is here to stay," she says proudly.

Still at the bottom of the steps, I suddenly think it best if I dash off into the fog and lose myself from this insane family.

"If you come live with us, you'll be forever changed, my dear," Ms. Christie says softly as she holds out her hand.

Aw, that woman wraps me around her little finger every time. What can I do but nod and accept her hand? The fog swallows up the front porch, but we are—I am—safe and sound inside.

———

Thanksgiving snuck up on me but not Ms. Christie or Vassy. Busy at the workshop and moving in with the Zimmermans, I have no time to check a calendar or to see Georgie or Samuel.

Mr. Winslow, however, questions me daily about my living at the boarding house, as if I'm not good enough or I'm a criminal. I'd stand up and shout at him for doing such a sneaky thing, tell Mr. Jack or his wife, but I'm not wanting the accountant to start looking into my past life. I'm not sure how a body goes about doing that, but if Lazarus Winslow can dig up dirt on all the men in the workshop, then he can find my secrets.

Best to ignore the man. He's the only blight on my days. For certain, the rest of my time is filled with making the tiny room next to Jackie's room my own. I protested the room; I thought I'd be on the first floor with the boarders, but Ms. Christie put me right up on the second floor with the family.

When the boarders found out, most of them raised an eyebrow or two but said nothing. Winslow, of course, hates that I'm here. Mr. Fuller, the one who owns the hardware store, tells me how lucky I am. He's a nice chap. Welcomes me to the boarding house. Claps me on the shoulder and shakes my hand, like I'm special and grown-up. But then he's like that. A nice person that you'd want to have for a friend.

Ms. Christie told the children that I'd be living with them. Jackie raced around gathering sheets and a pillow, delighted, it seemed, that I'm moving in. Louise didn't have much to say other than story time would be a lot more fun, which made Ms. Christie snort. She usually reads to the children.

"Seems I have a rival," she said that day.

So here I am, on the second floor, in a room of my own. From the quilts stored in the hall closet, I was allowed to pick out one I liked for my bed. I sit now on a blue and white quilt, one that makes me think of the gulf waters when the north wind blows, pushing the waves out away from shore. Otherwise, the waters up close to the beach tend to be greener.

"Jonathan?" Lawrence stands at my door.

"Come on in." I pat the bed beside me. The little fella scrambles up beside me but has to collect his breath before he can speak again.

We sit in companionable silence.

"Are you going to stay forever?" he asks at last.

"Well," I pause because *forever* truly is a long time. "I suppose I'll be like you and Jackie and Louise. Some day when we're all grown up, we'll find other things to do and move on. But this will always be home. And home is a really nice place to have waiting for you."

Lawrence sits without speaking for so long that I figure he's got nothing to add. But, as usual, when it comes to this little man, I'm wrong.

"I think Jackie will follow Papa into business. Louise will be like Mama."

"You mean get married to some nice man and have lots of babies?"

"Yes, like that." He stares for a few seconds, sort of lost in thought.

"And what about you?" I'm curious as to what he sees in his future.

"Oh, I don't know," he answers as he swings his feet against the side of the covers and stares off into space. "I don't think I'll grow up."

"Well, that's a mighty odd thing to say." What he says makes me stop and take a good look at him. The slight body, thin fair hair, pale skin. Almost as if he's sick. But he's not.

"It's just a feeling I get now and then. Like you said your friend Samuel gets." He hops off the bed and moves to the door. But the four-year old stops with one hand on the doorframe. "Time will tell, won't it, Jonathan?"

My chest suddenly squeezes tight. This little man should grow up to be a teacher or doctor...something fine and meaningful. But today, I have to agree with him, "Yes, Lawrence, time will tell."

————

Life at the boarding house ain't perfect. Mr. Jack and Ms. Christie snipe at each other now and then, especially when she lifts something too heavy for a lady expecting a baby. She fusses when he returns home well after dark, after helping his men deliver furniture that clients commissioned. Jackie and Louise get into hassles with each other. Each one can find a way to muss up Ms. Christie's day. Even Juliet dashes around the house, doing her chores, minus her usual smile now and then. Ms. Vassy burns the toast or chars up the meat once in a while.

But I look at it all in a bigger sense now—this is home, no matter how temporary—and no one's perfect. Life's a dang sight better here than it was with Maw tiptoeing around Paw when he had little money or was liquored up and mean. Fussing and bustling around here ain't nothing like that. So, I can live with it.

————

"Georgie! Samuel!" Both boys reached the beach before me. In the middle of December, weeks since I've seen either one of them, we embrace roughly, then stand around with our hands in pockets, hunkered down in coats. The wind off the water bites into my face, turns my ears numb.

"Jonathan!" Further up the beach, away from the water's edge, sits Casper, on the wagon seat of the Zimmerman Furniture delivery wagon. He waves, motioning me—us—to the wagon.

"Come on, fellas," I urge. I grab both by the arms. They don't know the surprise I have to tell them.

"This is Casper. He works for Mr. Jack. Casper, this is Georgie and Samuel." I introduce the three and hop up beside Casper. "Get in the back. Come on, Samuel. You, too. Mr. Jack and Ms. Christie are expecting all three of us, and you don't want to piss off that lady by not showing up."

"What about Sister? When she comes to pick me up?" Georgie says as he scrambles in the back and holds out his hand for Samuel.

"What about me being in the boarding house?" Samuel asks, his feet still firm on sand.

"You gonna pass up an invitation to see my new room and eat some of Ms. Vassy's cooking?" I throw out my surprise sooner than I wanted to.

"Room?" Both boys stutter.

"You bet!" Casper throws in. "Jonathan here lives with the Zimmermans now!"

"This is a good thing?" Samuel whispers.

"The best," I assure him. I offer my hand, and he finally takes it. Georgie and Samuel scoot up behind the wagon seat, so they can see where we're going. "First we have a delivery to make to St. Mary's in town as a matter of fact. Georgie, I bet that sister will be there, while she waits for the supplies. You can run in and leave a message that she can come for you at Zimmerman's boarding house on Avenue L. Samuel, walking down Avenue L will get you home quicker than walking along the streets like we usually do," I add.

"All in?" Casper asks.

"All in!" I yell with a grin.

To St. Mary's first where Georgie does indeed find the sister. Casper and I deliver a small hall table to the nuns, while the young fella asks the sister to meet him at the boarding house. Samuel waits in the wagon, his hands on the reins to calm the team.

Once we gather again, Casper turns the team toward home. "Cold enough today to freeze the arse end off a mule," he mumbles.

"Wait 'til you see my room," I turn to tell Georgie and Samuel. "Ms. Christie and Mr. Jack asked me to live with them after the fire burned

Mrs. Abbey's place. We've been so busy, and the weather's been rainy, so I settled in without being able to tell you two right off."

The three of us fall silent. No one has much to say about Mrs. Abbey's house burning or Willie's death.

"You seen Rowdy or Jason since that...?" Georgie has trouble saying *fire*. Maybe it's 'cause I could have been the one who died.

"Naw, ain't seen hide nor hair of 'em. I don't even know if they're still in Galveston any more. That fire could have scared them off. Maybe they went to Houston or someplace like that."

We chew on that for the rest of the ride. Soon enough Casper pulls up to the barn. Gerty and Hank, the team that pulls the big wagon, stomp and snort, eager to get inside the barn and out of the chill.

"Run along with you, young fellas. I'll take care of the team," Casper offers.

"Thanks, Casper!" I yell. Not one to stay when given an opportunity to leave, we race to the back yard of the boarding house. While I run up the back stairs two at a time—as if coming home—Georgie and Samuel skid to a stop on the brick pavers in the yard.

"Come on, fellas," I call at the screen door. Both stand, almost identical but for color. Eyes down, caps in hand, one foot swishing back and forth, like they ain't sure they're really welcomed or not.

"Jonathan?" Ms. Christie calls from the other side of the screen. She pushes it open and steps out beside me. "Good morning, Georgie. Samuel. Mighty fine to see you two visiting. Jonathan's been in a positive swivel wanting to get you two here."

"Aw, ma'am." Her words embarrass me even if they are true.

Her giggle is low. "Would you two like to see the Christmas tree we decorated last night?"

At that, Georgie's eyes get big as platters. Samuel's family always has a tree, and Georgie and I visit in order to see it, but neither one's seen a tree like *this* one.

"Come on, you two." I clomp back down the stairs and grab them by the jackets. "You gotta see this!"

Reluctantly Samuel follows Georgie and me into the big room just inside the door. Vassy uses the table in here to rest her vittles when she brings them in from the kitchen out-building. She stacks dirty dishes here. Ms. Christie dumps the dirty sheets and other things here in a basket. She calls this a 'utility room', one she uses for just about everything. To one side is a narrow stairway, leading up to the second floor. Juliet and Ms. Christie use it when doing chores, so as not to bother the boarders. Only Juliet uses it these days. Ms. Christie's too bulky to make it up the skinny staircase. Mr. Jack teases her about it all the time.

"You can hang your jackets in here, boys," she says. "Follow me and be prepared for a big surprise." She sails out of the room, headed to the parlor.

"You won't believe this tree," I whisper. "I ain't never seen anything like it."

By now, both boys have gotten over any reason to go slow. We shuck our jackets, and they follow me down the hall. I stop at the parlor door. "Middle of the day and everyone's gone to work. Well, Mr. Jones is sleeping down the hall. He works night shift at the docks. So, we all gotta be quiet, but the house is ours." I stand back and let them enter. Ms. Christie stands on the far side of the room next to the fireplace.

"Oh, Jonathan!" Georgie is all eyes, his mouth hanging agape.

"Man, what a tree!" Samuel says.

Indeed, the Zimmerman's Christmas tree is taller than anything I've ever seen. The ceilings are fourteen-foot tall, the better to circulate cool breezes in the summer heat. So, when Mr. Jack and Thomas brought in the tree, I thought it way too big. But naw, the star on top sits right beneath the ceiling; the tree is a perfect fit.

"Everyone decorated it," I tell them. "The boarders and the family."

"Even you?" Georgie whispers.

"Even Jonathan," Ms. Christie says, coming forward with her hands behind her back, her big belly leading the way. "Jonathan is part of our family now. And, as his best friends, you're always welcome here. He says you're the only two he'd want to come here. You'd not hurt the children or me."

A small brown head and a taller black-haired one nod so hard their teeth almost clank.

"Well then, gentlemen..." She holds out her hands, a decoration in each. "I think you should add an ornament, too."

Samuel steps back, while Georgie puts both hands behind his back.

"Ain't fittin', ma'am," Samuel says.

"I ain't nobody to put a thing on a fancy tree like that," Georgie says.

I feel like Mr. Jack...that day I agreed to stay here. Push them into a corner and let them wiggle.

Ms. Christie cocks her brow and gives each one a serious stare. "You're Jonathan's best friends, are you not?"

Both nod again.

"Then you'll be our best friends. Now..." She holds out the ornaments again. "Best friends share good times as well as bad. And this, gentlemen, is a good time. Come," she says as she reaches for Samuel's hand. Clasping it ever so softly, she leads him forward, then places a small bird made of colored glass in his hand. "So, you can't fly away from us," she whispers. "We'll let this pretty one do the flying for us." She guides his hand up but releases it when he reaches higher than her head. Easy as a cloud, he lowers the delicate ornament onto a branch, then fastens it there, so the bird looks real.

"Me next, ma'am."

I can't remember the last time I saw Georgie look so young or so eager. He speaks low, but he wiggles like a puppy waiting to be petted.

"Yes, you're next, Master Georgie," Ms. Christie says as she holds out a hand that he grasps eagerly. "And where would you like to put this tiny angel, sir?" She shifts the tiny gold and silver angel into his cupped hands. He holds it like a jewel, something rare and precious. He turns his attention to the tree, looking it over, studying it.

"Here, ma'am." He leans forward but hesitates.

"There would be perfect, sir," Ms. Christie encourages him. I breathe a sigh of relief. Both have become part of the family whether they know it or not. Oh, not to live here. But part of the warmth that defines those who are close. I wish Georgie could live here. He and Jackie would get along fine. But that's not to be. Georgie has his own place in life.

Samuel and Georgie step back and gaze at the tall Christmas tree, sighs of their own filling the room with happiness.

"This is even better than us having the same birthday," Georgie says.

"What?" Ms. Christie's hearing is like that of a well-bred dog...never misses a thing as I discovered one night when I read a story to Jackie past bedtime.

"Uh, nothing, ma'am," Georgie stammers. I'm sure he thinks he's said something wrong.

"I distinctly heard the word 'birthday', young man. Explain please," she demands...but in a nice way so as not to scare him, I'm sure.

"Well, you see, ma'am," he begins but turns frightened eyes on me.

"Along the way, Ms. Christie, Samuel, Georgie and I learned we have the same birthday. December fifteen."

"Why I declare! That's the most perfect thing." She claps her hands like a girl. "Oh! Oh!"

"What? What!" Her sudden shout sends me into a fit. "You're not having the baby, are you?" I move to her side, but she breaks out laughing. Patting my arm, she says, "No, not yet. But I just realized...today is December the fifteenth!"

"It is?" the three of us ask together. I never look at calendars, and I doubt Samuel does either. Georgie could care less what day it is.

"It certainly is! Happy Birthday!" She glides forward, plants a kiss on Samuel's cheek—he blushes so hard I can see it through his dark skin—kisses Georgie on the tip of his nose—he does that wiggle thing again—then she stops before me. Standing on her tiptoes, she plants a kiss on my cheek as well.

"That's such a nice turn to the day. When the children return from the workshop, I'll have to tell them. Oh!"

"What?" I can't help but ask.

"Not the baby, Jonathan. You worry too much," she tosses my direction. "Why don't the three of you walk down to the workshop and gather the children. They've been watching their papa carve a nut cracker statue that the mayor ordered for his children." She hustles us all down the hall again into the back room. "Won't they be surprised to see

Jonathan's visitors," she says as she buttons Georgie in his jacket and straightens the thin scarf around Samuel's neck. Before I can grab it, she hands me my cap. "Jonathan, bundle up the children well before they come outside, especially Lawrence." With that, she once more hustles us forward, straight out onto the back porch. "I'll ask Vassy to make some hot cocoa for all of you. Maybe she'll have some cookies we can add." And she waddles off toward the kitchen, while the three of us make our way out of the gate.

"That woman's something else," Samuel says as soon as we're far enough away he knows she won't hear him.

"She's a corker, all right," I add.

"I think she's wonderful," Georgie says.

Poor Georgie. He must be missing his maw right now. I know how he feels.

———

By four that afternoon, the sun is setting low across the west end. Shadows form over the tops of houses along the street.

Georgie and Jackie did indeed hit it off. They played with blocks, then Jackie read a story to Georgie, talking in the same silly voices I use when I read it. Meanwhile, Lawrence sits with Samuel and me as we visit, and I show him my room. Louise bounces in and out of my room and Jackie's, often going off to play with her dolls.

"This is a pretty one." Samuel holds up my favorite seashell.

"I found that late one day on the shore. Can't believe the waves didn't break it up. That was a few weeks back when we had that storm. Remember?"

"Yeah." He puts the shell back on the window ledge. "Paw couldn't go to work that day 'cause the street flooded. Mr. Waller docked him a day's wages."

"That's not fair! Mr. Perkins couldn't get to work through the high water," I argue.

"That might be, but Paw didn't argue. Can't afford to lose his job."

I fume at the injustice. Like ol' Winslow holding secrets over everyone's head at the workshop and no one brave enough to tell Mr. Jack. I steer clear of the accountant for that very reason.

"Have you seen Rowdy or Jason?" Samuel asks.

"Not since that last day."

"Odd that they disappeared like that."

"Yep. Guess we'll never know what happened to them."

"Maybe they got kilt, too," Lawrence says, his face full of concern.

"Hadn't thought of that, but they weren't in the fire, little man," I sit on the bed beside him and remind him. I forget now and then that he's a little fella and probably shouldn't hear worrisome things like that.

He gives an elaborate shrug. "Just a thought," he says, imitating his paw.

Samuel and I exchange looks. I wonder if he's thinking the same thing Lawrence mentioned. Are those two dead?

In the middle of our visit enters Juliet. "Jonathan, Ms. Christie says for all of you to come with me, including the children."

"Juliet, this here is Samuel Houston Perkins. That other fella with Jackie is Georgie. You remember them from the beach last spring?"

She drops a quick curtsey and nods. "I do remember. Nice to meet you, Samuel." She motions toward the stairs. "Y'all go down while I get the others."

"Come on, Lawrence."

The little boy sits on the bed, the quietest youngun' I've ever seen. Today he looks peeked, his face paler than normal.

"Wanna piggy back ride, little man," I lean down to ask.

"Yes, please," he answers. Neither of us question why I ask or he says yes.

I ease down on one knee, he slides on to my back, and I stand, my arms wrapped behind me, my hands locked under his rear in order to help him sit easier. "Here we go."

At the top of the stairs, we wait for the others to join us.

Two men step through the front door. Mr. McGraw and Mr. Thrill, the railroad men, must have just come in on the afternoon train. They see us gathered at the top of the stairs. Their usual smiles of greeting turn to frowns. They've spotted Samuel.

Quick like a tern running along the edge of the waves looking for something to eat, I devise a plan to get us all downstairs without meeting the disapproval of those two bigots.

"Race you," I tell Georgie, Jackie and Louise. "Samuel, Lawrence and I will take the back stairs. You take these, and I bet we beat you."

"No, you won't!" Jackie yells. "Come on, Georgie, Lou!" Like a herd of cattle, they rattle down the stairs.

"Race you," I tell Samuel and make for the back stairs. As narrow as they are, I let Samuel go first while Lawrence encourages me as if he's the rider of a racehorse.

The little guys beat us but not by much. Juliet is the judge since she's standing by the back door. "The winners," she taps Jackie, Georgie and Louise on the tops of their heads.

Those three jump around and shout like crazy folk, while Lawrence drops his forehead against my head and groans over their silly antics.

"Come on now, or the surprise will be cold," Juliet urges us outside.

"What surprise?" Lawrence leans around my shoulder, throwing me a bit off balance.

"You gotta wait and see," is all Juliet will say. She heads to the kitchen.

"Ta da!" she says and throws open the kitchen door. We waltz in but stop in a clutter when we see a huge cake sitting on the center counter. Ms. Christie and Vassy stand behind the counter, grinning from ear to ear.

"What do you think?" Ms. Christie asks us.

"What is that?" Georgie creeps forward to examine the cake.

"Why, it's a birthday cake, sir!"

"What?" As if we'd practice, we all speak at once.

Vassy grins and starts laying out plates and cups of milk. "This here is a birthday cake for Mr. Jonathan, Mr. Samuel there and little Mr. Georgie."

I can tell Georgie is about to cry. Samuel looks flabbergasted. I can't talk; something's blocking my throat.

"Come on, all of you. Pull up a stool, and let's celebrate." Ms. Christie starts to lift Louise onto a stool, but Samuel gets there first. "Pardon, Miss Louise," he says as he places the little girl on the tall stool. "You got no business lifting so much, ma'am."

"Thank you, Samuel. You're right, of course."

I ease Lawrence onto a stool and help Jackie get on his. The rest of us pull up a stool, sit and wait.

"I never had a birthday cake," Georgie whispers, his eyes glued to the cake plates Vassy's passing around.

"Can Juliet have some, too?" I have to ask. She's standing by the door, her eyes showing how much she'd like to join us.

"Oh, Juliet, dear heart. Of course, you must join us. We're celebrating!" Ms. Christie waddles over and pulls Juliet on to a stool next to me.

I won't look at her, and she's not looking at me, but I'm glad she's here with us.

When we all have our cake, Ms. Christie holds up her hands for attention. "I'm not sure if everyone—anyone's—ever heard this song before but let me sing it to you."

In a voice not like an angel exactly or a croaking frog either, she sings:

Happy Birthday to you.
Happy Birthday to you.
Happy Birthday, dear Jonathan, Samuel and Georgie,
(She almost runs out of air, she has so many to name)
Happy Birthday to you!

Rousing applause greets her enthusiastic song.

Our mouths full, the kitchen is silent but for the clink of forks against plates. Even Ms. Christie and Vassy have a piece of chocolate cake.

"This is better than my maw makes," Samuel says, a crumb stuck to the side of his mouth.

"That's saying a lot, Ms. Vassy. His maw is a great cook," I tell the woman.

"Better than Christmas," Georgie mutters as he devours his second piece.

"Better than any Christmas ever, little fella," I agree as I ruffle his hair.

"Gentlemen," Ms. Christie pauses to amend, "Samuel and Georgie—you're welcome back any time. Now Juliet, Vassy and I have chores to do. Jonathan has to help with deliveries. So, before we go our separate ways, I'll wish you all a Merry Christmas."

Warmed by more than just a stove, the very spirit of the season rises to the rafters as we all call out, "Merry Christmas!"

——————

With only three days left before Christmas, I stop by Mr. Johnson's green grocery to get a few extra dollars from the money he holds for me. I want to buy Christmas presents. Not big things. I can't afford such, but little things that each person will enjoy.

"Pssst," comes from my right. I look around but see no one. Guess I imagined that noise. I take two steps and hear 'pssst' again. This time I catch a hand waving at me from the alley next to the grocery.

Being late in the day and having a little money on me, I question whether or not to follow the hand that's urging me closer.

"Jonathan," someone calls softly. The hand is replaced by...Rowdy?

I hurry around the corner and down the alley until I join up with my former roommates, Rowdy and Jason.

"Where have you two been? We thought you might have been killed, too."

"Yeah, we know. Like Willie," Jason hisses. He looks around like someone's after him.

"Why you so jumpy?"

"Someone is maybe after us," Rowdy answers as he pulls me deeper into shadows.

73

"How come?"

"Mind you, we didn't have no idea what was going to happen." Rowdy's defending himself and Jason, but I don't know why.

"Tell me," I urge because they look like horses about to bolt.

"This guy approached us that afternoon—"

"The afternoon before the fire?"

"Yeah, he gave us each ten dollars to play a trick on you. All innocent-like, see?"

"Who was he, and why'd you trust him?"

"Hey, Jon, boy, someone says he's gonna give you more money than you've seen in a year, you gonna turn him away?" Jason sounds defensive but looks guilty as all get out.

"So, what happened?"

"He tells us to make sure you're in the bedroom, then to lock the door so you can't get out."

"He say why?"

"No. Just said to keep our eyes open and if anything backfired on the joke that we were to make sure everyone was safe." This time Rowdy not only looks guilty but a bit sick.

"So, you asked Mrs. Abbey if I was in for the night? Right?"

"Yeah." Jason's answering 'cause Rowdy's gone to the corner to see if anyone's around.

"She said I was, so you locked the bedroom door," I guessed.

"How was we to know that it was Willie in there and not you. Damn ol' woman gets you two mixed up all the time," Jason complains.

"And you know it, too. Never thought to check, did you?" I have little sympathy for the two. Someone bought them off. I'm ready to leave these two but want more information.

"When the fire started, what did you two do?"

"We were talking to Mrs. Abbey, in the kitchen, waiting to laugh at you trying to get out of the door when the 'joke' happened. Suddenly the whole back end of the house sort of exploded. No way could we get back there. We went around the other end of the hall and managed to get the other fellas out."

"No one's seen them since the fire, but the police told Mr. Jack that they're all safe, and none had anything to do with the fire."

"Fire, my foot," Rowdy exclaimed quietly. "That place went up like a tinderbox. Some joke. Only after everyone was out did we think this wasn't so funny, but we'd already taken the money and thrown the lock on that door. If anyone says anything, we'll go to jail."

"Or worse," Jason adds, a sheen of sweat covering his face even in the December chill.

"So where have you been since then?"

"Hiding out down along east beach. But we gotta get away."

Immediately I figure they're after money to help them leave. "Look, fellas—" I begin.

"We're headed to Houston on the train. Figure Christmas day we can get lost in the crowds going there to visit. Not sure but we think that guy is after us. We didn't hold up our part of the bargain, I 'spect." By now, both fellas are a bit green-looking.

"But you gotta tell the police what happened. That someone paid you to do all that. Willie died!" I yell. "That could have been me!" I remind them with a growl.

"It would have been too bad if that had been you," Rowdy says rather cold-heartedly. "But seeing as it was Willie that died in that fire, then good riddance."

"You don't know!" It dawns on me that these two think Willie died in the fire; he didn't.

"Know what?"

"Willie was dead before the fire. Someone bashed him in the head. Killed him and left him in my bed. Our bed," I pass a finger back and forth between Jason and me.

"Kilt? Before the fire?"

"Oh, man!" Jason really looks sick now. "We gotta get outta here."

"I ain't talking to no police either," Rowdy hisses.

"If you don't go see 'em, at least call, and tell them what happened," I urge them. "You didn't kill Willie. You was just paid to play a joke on me. You didn't know a guy would use you to help him murder someone."

Nervous as two cats in a roomful of big-footed guys, the two cut glances at each other. Rowdy shrugs. "I don't know."

"Look, we're headed out of town. Someone's been following us for two days now. If he killed Willie before the fire, he might kill us and not bother with a fire. We'll be just as dead," Jason reasons.

"At least think about calling the police. You can do it from the station just before your train leaves."

They begin pulling away, headed for the front of the alley.

"At least think about it."

"Maybe we will," comes back in a whisper from Rowdy.

"Good luck, fellas," I call back but quiet-like in case someone else is listening.

But I hear nothing from them. They've scampered off to who knows where.

I head home too, walking faster than I normally would. Someone paid to have me killed.

Should I tell the Zimmermans or just leave?

———

Home is too dear to me now. I can't leave. But I can't put the family in danger if someone's still trying to kill me. And why would they? I'm nobody.

Still I need a cooler head for advice. Taking a chance that I might be kicked out of the house anyway, I corner Mr. Jack late one evening. He's still in his office at the workshop, ready to close it up for Christmas Eve. The entire household had a magnificent dinner at noon. Vassy outdid herself. With the dishes washed and the kitchen clean, the Zimmermans sent Vassy and Juliet home with their gifts. Only the family and two boarders, Lazarus Winslow and Mr. Fuller, remain at the house. Mr. McGraw and Thrill drew the holiday shift on the train. As senior supervisor at the docks, Mr. Jones took two days off to go to Houston to see his parents. Before late night church services begin, Mr. Jack wants to see that the workshop is ship-shape. He won't open again until the day after Christmas.

"Sir?" I call out quietly so as not to startle the man.

"Jonathan? Come in. What brings you here?" Mr. Jack closes the book on his desk, shoves it in a drawer and pushes back his chair.

"Finished, sir?"

He nods. "I was putting the last book away when you came." He pauses, then nods toward the chair at the side of his desk. "Why don't you sit? You look like a man with something on his mind."

I sit and nod like he does. But how can I tell him what I know?

"Spit it out, son. Can't be any worse than keeping all those worries bottled up inside."

Once again, he reads my mind. Am I so easy to read? If so, I'd make a terrible poker player.

"Sir..." I swallow. This ain't going to be easy. "Sir, remember my two roommates, Rowdy and Jason?"

"No one's seen them since the fire."

"I saw them two days ago. They had some interesting things to say."

"Like what?" His attention caught, Mr. Jack leans forward, his elbows on his knees, his hands clasped.

"Some man paid them ten dollars apiece to lock the door to my bedroom and keep me there while he played a 'joke' on me."

"Good Lord!"

"Yes, sir. They did it, too. Came in, asked Mrs. Abbey if I was in the room and locked the door. And Willie died in my place."

"Because the old woman got you and that other young man confused, thought Willy was you."

"Yes, sir. Rowdy said the man told them to make sure everyone was safe when he played the joke...which turned out to be some kind of explosion." My stomach turns over, and I swallow. I can get sick too easy telling this story. "When the back of the house exploded, they got everyone...but Willie...out."

"So, they had no idea Willie died instead of you."

"It wasn't until later that they learned that. And not until we met up

77

that they found out that Willie was dead before the fire started."

"Are they going to tell the police what happened?"

"Jason said a man was following them. They'd been hiding out. But they were going to hop a train to Houston in order to escape...hopefully."

"They need to call the police!"

"I told them that. They said maybe."

"So, they're gone now?"

"I reckon so."

"Nothing you can do about it, son," Mr. Jack says as he comes around the desk and lays a hand on my shoulder.

"But if someone tried to kill me—only it was Willie instead—then that man might still be after me," I'm trying to make him understand. "The family might be in danger, sir." I finally look up at him, directly into his eyes. "Maybe it's best if I leave, so nobody gets hurt."

Mr. Jack stands there, giving me the most peculiar look. "You...you expect us to just let you go? Let you leave our home? Our family?" He seems appalled by the idea. His hand tightens slightly on my shoulder as if keeping me in place.

"Well, yes, sir. I ain't one for bringing hurt to you or Ms. Christie or the little ones." He just won't understand my worries.

"Son, let me explain how a family works." He pulls the chair in front of the desk over in front of me. "Families don't abandon members when the going gets tough."

A memory flashes through my mind. "Yes, sir...they do sometimes."

But he keeps talking. "We stick together, and if there's trouble, we face it together. My wife will tell you the same thing." He winks to assure me Ms. Christie is not about to let me go.

"But what about the children? What if someone tries to hurt them?"

"They won't."

"But—"

"Son, we'll handle any problem together the same as if it were mine or Ms. Christie's or Vassy's or Jackie's. That's what families do. You can't leave. We simply won't let you." He grins and pats my knee. "Now what about changing clothes, so we can drive to church?"

"But, sir, you trust me? You still want me to stay?" Like Samuel on our birthday, now I'm flabbergasted.

"Of course we want you to stay, silly boy!" He pulls me up and hooks an arm through mine. Walking me to the workshop door, he holds on to me as he pulls it shuts, locks it and pockets the key. "Now, no more talk of leaving. We shall inform my wife of your concern after Christmas. But be warned, she will brook no mention of you leaving. You, Jonathan Evans," he grins as he informs me, "are stuck with us!"

———

A scream pierces the dusk. Ms. Christie went upstairs hours earlier, leaving us to put out the candles on each branch of the Christmas tree that still stands in the parlor even though it's New Year's Eve.

"I'm not feeling myself tonight, Jonathan," she apologized at the time. We'd sat opposite each other over Mr. Jack's checker table. She had taught me how to play, and I was contemplating my next moves when she stirred as if uncomfortable in her chair.

Immediately I stood, concern making my heart beat harder. "You gonna be all right, ma'am?" I know she heard the worry in my voice.

"Indeed, sir. If you'll find Mr. Jack, I think I'll lean on his arm going up the stairs."

Frozen in place, I debated leaving her or offering my arm. Her huge middle looked even larger in the glow of the electric lights behind her. I imagined the babe within wiggling, much like the tiny girl child did when Maw was about to birth her.

"You aren't...?" No way would I ask what I was thinking.

"I'm fine, Jonathan. No need for worry." Her voice low so the men in the room wouldn't hear, she patted my arm. "Now skedaddle. Find Mr. Jack. I think he's upstairs reading to the children."

Without ado, she actually shoved me to get me moving.

That was three hours ago.

Two hours ago, Juliet came pounding down the stairs. "Jonathan! Jonathan!" Her voice carried through the house. I imagined the boarders waking, wondering whether the house was afire. I remember shivering, a house on fire being too close a memory for comfort.

"What? Is Ms. Christie—?"

Juliet interrupted me. "She's having her baby! Mr. Jack said you have to get Granny Krenshaw right now! Hurry!" She pushed me toward the door, grabbing my jacket off the coat rack.

"What's going on?" Lazarus Winslow poked his head around the edge of the doorframe from the hall leading to the boarders' rooms.

"Ms. Christie's having her baby. Jonathan's going for the midwife," Juliet told him in one breathless rush. "Go back to bed," she ordered. For a maid of fifteen, she had no business telling a boarder that sort of thing, but to my surprise, Winslow tucked his head back. I heard him padding down the hall.

"Jonathan!" Juliet yelled at me again. "Hurry!"

Mr. Jack prepared me for this—getting the midwife. He drove me by her house one day not two weeks ago. "I'll be with Ms. Christie. You'll be the one to get Granny Krenshaw. It's an important job, son. The most important one."

I remember giving him a look like 'I don't think so' before he realized what he said and winked. "Well, not the most important one. I think that belongs to my wife...and maybe the midwife. But you understand."

I did understand. Having someone that knew what was going on was urgent. I wished when Maw...

"You're daydreaming. Skedaddle!" Juliet shoved me between the shoulders, pushing me on to the porch.

An hour ago, the moans started. Each one got louder. By that time, even the boarders were awake. Several of the men didn't want to hang around and lose a night's sleep—much less listen to a woman giving birth —so they headed for the train station. Winslow threw on a coat and announced, "I'm spending the night at the office."

Good riddance to them all.

And now the screams.

I'm afraid, but with the children huddled around me and Juliet, I can't show it. Juliet got the fire going in the parlor, while Granny

Krenshaw worked upstairs. After I returned with the midwife, I made a dash down the island for Vassy. Thankfully, old Gerty let me harness her to the buggy without fuss. She's not a mean-tempered horse. Just likes to remind us that she's the boss.

Vassy's husband answered the door of their tiny house. Like me, he understood how important Vassy was to us at this time. He hustled her into the buggy after giving her a kiss. "I'll be back when I can, Wilson," she told him as she scooted closer to me. I forgot to bring a blanket to cover our legs, and the night air was sharp with chill.

Vassy prepares hot water and hauls that and bundles of towels up the stairs. At one point, she begins a hot meal I doubt anyone will eat until this baby is born. "Something simple," she says. Never did she ask Juliet to leave the children. The maid holds Louise, while Jackie huddles on one side of me and Lawrence on the other.

How I wish I could take them somewhere else. Listening to your maw scream in pain is frightening enough. Listening for hours as the sun comes up over the gulf is far too long for anyone to endure. I've been there. I know.

Suddenly the screams turn into the loudest grunts I've ever heard. Almost like growls. Is that good? What do *those* sounds mean? If we were afraid earlier, we're terrified now. As long as Ms. Christie screams, we know she's still here. These growls and grunts tell us nothing.

I concentrate so hard on listening to those noises from up the stairs that when they stop, I blink. No sound. No gulf-borne breeze rattling the metal chime on the front porch. No screams, grunts or growls. The silence is profound after listening to those sounds and the pounding of my own heart for hours. What's happening?

The children are asleep, though how they can sleep through those nerve-wracking sounds I'll never know. Juliet and I glance at each other, then back toward the parlor doorway.

"How's Ms. Christie—?" Vassy enters, and we jump.

"Shhhh!" I hiss at her. "Listen!"

Vassy cocks her head to one side and closes her eyes. Her way of concentrating, I suppose.

But there's nothing to hear. That scares me more than anything else I've heard. The sound of nothing.

Then into that silence creeps a tiny noise. A soft whisper of a sound. Light. Delicate. A hiccup of awakening. A voice new to the world of cold and light. Without warning, those soft snuffles turn into full-throated howls. The baby has arrived!

But we're not fools. A baby is one thing...the mother? Did both survive the birthing?

"It's a girl! Mother and baby are fine!" comes a deep joyous shout from above. Mr. Jack! Announcing the birth of another daughter and the glad news that both child and mother are all right.

I literally collapse back onto the pile of divan cushions I'd stacked behind me hours before. My heart races but with relief this time. Still...a corner of my mind worries that one or both might not survive the day or the night or even the next.

Still I'll worry about that if necessary. For now, Juliet, Vassy and I giggle and laugh loud enough that we wake the children. Jackie is old enough to understand that another baby has arrived. The twins are just now five, and I'm not sure if they realize they're not the darling youngest any more. *Darling* yes but no longer the youngest.

Jackie dances around the floor, assured his mother is all right. Louise hugs Juliet and snuggles in her lap.

"Mama's going to be all right, isn't she, Jonathan?" Lawrence, ever the one for deep thinking, is like me in that respect. Will Ms. Christie be all right?

"I think so, Lawrence. Granny Krenshaw is the best midwife there is," I assure him though Mr. Jack had to assure me not long ago.

"Another girl?" the little fella asks.

"Yep."

"Can I play with her? I'll share my blocks with her," Lawrence offers quietly.

I curl an arm around his back and pull him just a little closer. The little guy is worried that his maw won't love him anymore, I bet. "She might be a bit too tiny right now to play with your blocks, but your mama will be happy to see you sharing when she's old enough. Your mama loves you very much. But for a little while, this baby will need lots of attention. She can't do anything like you can yet. You're a big fella. She's just a tiny thing."

"Can I help Mama take care of the baby?"

"I bet your mama would love that," I try to assure him.

A soft sigh escapes the boy, and I hug him closer. Of all the children, he needs to know he's still loved and wanted.

Ever the one to keep priorities straight, Vassy says, "I have biscuits and jam with glasses of milk. I'll just bring them here into the parlor, so no one has to leave. Might be awhile before Mr. Jack comes down."

Juliet hops up. "I'll help." Louise holds out her hand. "Me, too. I'll help."

"Right you are, Miss Louise. You can carry the jam pot," Vassy says.

The trio of ladies leave, and us boys huddle nearer the fireplace. The morning is damp and overcast. Just like Ms. Christie said it would be three days earlier. I'm beginning to think she's more predictable at weather forecasting than Mr. Cline and the weather service down at the Levy building.

Vassy and her troops arrive soon enough with enough food to feed a small army. How she managed to cobble together a meal of fruit, biscuits, jam and cold milk while racing up and down the stairs all night is a mystery to me. She pulls the low table in front of one of the divans out into the middle of the room and sets out plates, glasses, knives and spoons. Juliet pours the milk, while Vassy prepares plates for the children.

I sit, useless in this situation, it appears. I'm the first to see a dark shadow stop just outside the parlor door. A shadow that dissolves into a man. A man holding a bundle. A silent but wiggling bundle.

The others haven't spotted Mr. Jack yet, but he and I catch each other's eye. He jerks his head, motioning me over. As I approach, he eases back into the dim light of the hallway, so it's only the three of us.

"My daughter," he whispers proudly, tilting his arms so I can see her. Suddenly a ray of soft light eases through the transom over the front door and shines on the baby's face. She quickly closes her eyes. Her paw turns slightly, so the light no longer falls directly on her, and she opens her eyes again.

My eyes are leaking. Tears! I've not cried in years! But I am now.

Ashamed, I duck my head and take a furtive swipe at my eyes to erase the tracks. But Mr. Jack's quick. He sees, and maybe he realizes how important this tiny child is. To his family and maybe to me.

"Want to hold her?" he asks even as he's easing the bundle from his arms to mine that open automatically.

Memories flood my mind. Maw and my baby sister. How near to death the one was. How beautiful the other was. I bury my face in the child's blanket. She wiggles, so I raise my head to see her—watching me! Watching...like she knows me! A hand makes its way out of the blanket and taps my chin. Oh, I know she's only hours old and knows not what she's doing, but still...

I cry. Softly into the whiteness that surrounds her. "Mattie...Mattie May." I can't help the memories.

"Mattie?" Mr. Jack doesn't try to take back his child. He hovers close but allows me time to gather myself. "You called her Mattie. Do you know someone with that name?" he asks quietly.

"Maw had a little girl. Said she'd call the baby Mattie May if it was a girl."

"Where are they now?"

"Heaven, I suppose."

"Oh, Jonathan, I'm so sorry. What happened?"

"Maw had a tough time. No midwife like Ms. Christie has. I suppose things went sideways. Paw never talked about it. I stayed in the front room, being a little shaver at the time. Maw screamed like Ms. Christie did. But when she got quiet I figured the baby was here. I stuck my head into the room. Blood." I shiver at the pictures in my mind. "Blood everywhere. Paw did his best, but Maw died birthing the baby."

"What happened to the little girl? To Mattie May?"

"She lived a day. But she was too little to make it on her own." I can't talk loud; my throat is too full of tears. "But she looked like this little one.

Bright eyes, dark hair. Round face." I bury my face once again in the blankets, taking in that unique baby smell, and I'm rewarded with a tap of her fingers against my ear. As I raise my head, a miracle occurs. Tiny ones this new aren't supposed to do things like smile yet; I know that. But this one...she looks right at me and lifts the corners of her mouth. Just like a real smile.

"Oh my, I think she likes you," Mr. Jack says with a chuckle.

That baby girl and I stare at each other for the longest time.

I love a good smoke. I love this family—I just now realize that. But my heart belongs to this tiny one who I fall in love with the minute she smiles at me.

"You and me, Mattie May. Just you and me," I whisper, contentment settling for the first time in my heart. "Now go to your papa." I ease the bundle—reluctantly—back into her father's arms. "Guess it's time to let the others see her, huh?"

"I think that's a good idea, son. Oh, and Jonathan, happy New Year," Mr. Jack replies as we step into the parlor doorway together, joined by an immediate unconditional love for this girl child.

———

I sit here alone in the parlor, watching another winter storm pass over the island. This new year...this new century...seems no different than the last year. A thought flits through my mind as I hear Juliet coming down the stairs and baby Mattie gurgling and cooing.

Mattie—how surprised was I when Mr. Jack and Ms. Christie invited the children...and me...into the sitting room upstairs and presented Matilda Marie Zimmerman to us all...to be called Mattie. I choked up, and they knew it. Waiting to one side of the room for my turn to hold little Mattie, I watched the others as Mr. Jack offered the baby to each, to hold.

Jackie held her for a few minutes, but a baby just lies there and isn't a lot of fun.

Louise sang to her, then lost interest.

Lawrence, the little thinker that always amazes me, sat on the divan, a pillow on his lap like the other two. When Mr. Jack laid Mattie on the pillow, the little boy solemnly counted her toes and fingers. He smoothed the dark hair that lay in fluffy curls on her head around her ears. He tapped her cheek and nose. She wiggled, and he grinned. Totally lost in the world of himself and that baby, he bent close and whispered to her. What he said none of us will ever know. We never asked, and he never said. But it was an earnest discussion. She focused on him, never wavering her attention. Perhaps she liked the sound of his voice.

Vassy and Juliet had their turn as well. Vassy's children are grown and live off the island. Juliet has sisters and brothers so knows how to hold a baby. She rocked gently back and forth...I think she had no idea she was doing it. She looked so pretty in her dark skirt and pale pink blouse with tiny tucks on it. Her long hair hung down, held away from her face by two barrettes that I gave her for Christmas.

When the children disappeared to the nursery and Vassy and Juliet returned to the kitchen and chores, Mr. Jack called me over to the divan. Ms. Christie sat in a chair next to it.

"You're the more grown-up member of the family, Jonathan. We didn't think you'd mind waiting until last." With that, he slipped that tiny girl into my arms.

The feel of soft material wrapped around a tiny body, the feel of her squirming to get comfortable in a new pair of arms. The smell of baby powder Ms. Christie uses on her.

"Hello, Mattie May," I remember saying automatically. Realizing that wasn't her name—her middle name being Marie and not May—I apologized without looking up. "Sorry. Wrong name. It'll take a bit to get that straight."

Just then, she lifted those lips again in a faint smile and gurgled. The first sounds I'd heard her make other than crying to be fed or changed.

"I don't think she minds," Ms. Christie said. "Would you mind holding her, while Mr. Jack helps me back to bed? You can bring her in when I'm settled."

She really gave me no time to answer as she stood and took her husband's arm. She moved stiffly but seemed all right. Mattie pulled my attention back to her again.

Like Lawrence, I talked to her. Silly talk to entertain.

That little girl has me wrapped around her tiny fingers for sure, with her smiles and wiggles and gurgles.

———

Winter finally gives way. Georgie, Samuel and I often meet at the beach. We're a brotherhood of three, stronger for the bond we share.

Once again, we meet, this time on a fine spring Saturday, almost a year to the day when we met the Zimmermans. I'd just started working for them. Now Georgie and Samuel come regularly to the house. Winter isn't the time to walk on beaches or test the warmth of the gulf waters, Ms. Christie told us after Christmas. She made it clear that the three of us could meet up at the house any time.

During the winter, we celebrated three more birthdays at the boarding house. Jackie turned seven and the twins turned five. Seems Ms. Christie likes having winter babies.

But today is too nice to pass up. I'm carrying the heavy picnic basket and oversized umbrella—what Ms. Christie calls a beach umbrella. Georgie carries a pile of blankets on his head, native style. We had to practically beg Samuel to join us. He showed up, and Mr. Jack clapped him on the shoulder, grinning like a fool, saying that our family was now complete. He's carrying a wooden box filled with pitchers of drink, lemonade mostly. Vassy makes the best lemonade. Juliet carries another box with plates, forks and spoons.

Jackie and Louise race around us, while Lawrence seems content to walk with Ms. Christie. Mr. Jack carries Mattie. She'll rest on a pile of blankets under the umbrella I'll stick into the sand.

What a day! Food, fun, family, friends. We swim, Georgie swallowing a gutful of salt water at one time. Mr. Jack stuck his finger down Georgie's throat and made him throw up the water. After that, the young fella sat under the umbrella.

Mr. Jack and his wife have loads of friends, and most of them are on the beach today. Seems like every few minutes someone comes over to say howdy and shake hands. Mr. Jack is faithful about introducing each of us, including Samuel.

As the afternoon winds down, Vassy packs up the picnic basket and boxes with drinks and dirty plates. We all came in the big furniture wagon that Mr. Jack left parked further up on the sandy beach, the horses tethered with water and oats. Samuel and I carry the heavy boxes back to the wagon.

When the sun begins to set, we'll pile back on the wagon, make a big swing through town, past Juliet's home, Vassy's home and Samuel's. Each of them protested the need, but as usual, the Zimmermans simply act out of the kindness of their hearts, taking care of those they feel close to. Protests died before we even took to the wagon that morning. The children look forward to sitting in the back on boxes, seeing the sights as we ride along.

"Night, Samuel," we call and wave to Mr. and Mrs. Perkins who watch from the door.

"Home, darling?" Mr. Jack asks his wife.

"Yes, please. I think this family is a bit tired," Ms. Christie says as she glances at me. I in turn glance at Jackie, Louise and Lawrence, all snuggled up against the cooler night air. All sleep peacefully. Georgie rests among them; he's spending the night at the Zimmermans. Sister will pick him up early the next morning. He's so excited. All four of them younguns' will probably wake up full of energy, ready to play all night when we get home. I hope not. I'm tired.

"We've a full house tonight, my dear," Ms. Christie says as she cuddles Mattie. The baby is more alert these days. Looks around, grins when she sees our faces and hunts for us when she hears our voices.

"This day has been the most perfect yet," Mr. Jack tells his wife. "I think 1900 will be an exceptional year."

———

"Look out!"

"Awwww!" Timbers crash around me. One hits my head, and the world fades.

"Jonathan!" Someone shakes me. "Jonathan Evans, you wake up this minute!"

"Darling, you might kill him shaking him like that. Give him time."

Behind my closed eyes, I hear voices. I recognize them all but for the deep one. But the pain...something hurts somewhere on me.

"Stand aside, please," that voice says. Hands run from my head down my chest, out my arms and to my fingers. Then they return to press on my chest, my hips and on down my legs. When those hands reach my right ankle, I jump back into waking with a scream.

"He screams like a girl," Jackie says in disgust.

"He screams like a young man upon whom a load of timbers fell. Now hold your tongue, young man," the deep voice reprimands.

"Yes, sir."

"Jackie, take your sister and brother to your rooms, please. Stay there."

"But, sir, will Jonathan be all right?" That's Lawrence, watching out for me.

"Yes, son. But I think his ankle is either broken or badly sprained. He needs rest, not a group hanging over him. You can see him in the morning. Will that do?"

"Yes, sir." Small feet come closer. A hand rests on my arm briefly. "See you tomorrow, Jonathan."

"How bad is it, Dr. Turner?" Mr. Jack asks.

"The large bone right at the ankle is broken. With rest and gentle activity, in a few weeks he'll be up and around as good as new."

I have to know. I reach out and catch the doc's arm. "Promise?"

"Bless my soul. Welcome back, young man. Yes, I promise." He pats my hand but firmly removes it.

Time slips by for me in a fog as he sets the bone and bandages it. By the time he leaves, I feel like an old man, sweating and hurting.

"Jonathan, are you in pain, dear?" Ms. Christie has slipped back into

89

my room.

"Some, ma'am." Can a broken bone in the foot hurt as much as birthing a baby? I don't think so.

"Here." She holds my head up and places a tiny pill on my tongue. She waits until I finish sipping water before laying me down again. "I'll just sit here awhile until you get to sleep," she says.

"No need," I tell her, but the pill is acting fast. My tongue already feels all fuzzy and thick.

"Rest."

Before sleep and that pill take me off, I think back to that accident. Timbers are always lashed down tight and secure when they're in the workshop. For this very reason. Mr. Jack doesn't want anyone to get hurt. So how come those timbers came loose just as I was cleaning up that area today?

———

By early summer I'm back to work, my ankle as good as new, just like the doc said. Mr. Jack says those timbers coming loose was an accident. Maybe, but from now on I'm keeping a close eye on goings-on around Zimmerman's Furniture workshop.

One afternoon Casper approaches Mr. Jack. "Can I speak with you, sir?" Mr. Jack grins and motions for Casper to speak, but the man adds, "In private, sir."

Pretty unusual for a worker to speak to the boss that way. As Mr. Jack and Casper head to the office with its closed door, I haul tail outside and camp out under the window. Nothing next to that window but a narrow alley and high wooden fence. I'm secure unless someone comes there, but this alley is out of the way. I'm safe for now. But Mr. Jack will have my hide if he catches me eaves dropping.

"What can I do for you, Casper?" I imagine Mr. Jack offering Casper the chair in front of his desk.

"I uh...I uh...I gotta..." Casper has troubles speaking. Not like him at all.

"Out with it, man." Mr. Jack encourages.

"I gotta quit, Mr. Jack."

"What?" That's the last thing Mr. Jack expected. Me, too. But my mind flashes back to Mr. Winslow who's been buzzing around the workshop lately instead of staying in his office. In fact, he was out of his tiny hole of an office the day those timbers fell.

"Casper, why is this happening? How long have you been with me?"

"Long time, Mr. Jack. But that don't make no never-mind. I gotta quit. We gotta leave Galveston."

Does Casper hang his head? Or look Mr. Jack straight in the eyes?

A chair scraps, and I know Mr. Jack has moved that one beside his desk over next to Casper. "Tell me what's going on."

"Someone's gonna tell you soon enough, sir. But I wanted to tell you before that. Won't make things any different, but you've always been fair to me, and you're entitled to that now."

"Go on."

"Back in the old days when I was young and...well, young and stupid, I worked for a big lumber company. Weren't here. Was in New Orleans. Company went bust...'cause of me."

"How so?"

"I kept the books. My paw taught me how. He told the company boss I was smart and could do the job."

Casper's chair creaks as if he's uncomfortable.

"My paw fell ill. I had no money, so I..."

"You took some from the company?" Mr. Jack finishes.

"Yes, sir. Embezzlement is what they call it. But no one knew."

"Then why are you leaving? I don't understand."

"I left and made it look like I was killed in a fire. Was an old street bum that I dragged over to the timbers and burned. He was dead when I found him...died of likker. I gave the money to Paw and lit a shuck out of town. Came to Galveston, met a pretty girl and married her, then got a job with you here. I been here lots of years, sir."

Neither Mr. Jack nor Casper speak for a few minutes. The silence kills me. I dare not sneak a peek into the room.

"You broke the law and never paid for it." Mr. Jack pretty well sums up Casper's problem.

"Yes, sir. And someone's found out. Threatens to get the New Orleans' authorities on to me." Casper stands, moves toward the door. "I've got kids and two grand boys now. My wife knew what I did before we married. She forgave me, knowing the Lord won't. A man's been squeezing money out of me for a long time now, but I'm about bled dry. I can't pay. When I can't no longer pay up what he asks, he'll call the police, and they'll arrest me. I can't die in jail, Mr. Jack. I can't embarrass my family now for something I did forty years ago. I wanted you to know it ain't nothing you done wrong that makes me leave. You and your missus been the best thing ever happened to me outside my family."

"Casper, wait!"

A door slams. I best skedaddle back to the workshop before someone catches me listening where I ain't supposed to be.

Casper flies past me as I round the corner. He narrowly misses knocking me down. "Sorry there, young fella," he says as he leaves.

I can't say a thing; I'm not supposed to know a thing. What I do know is the identity of the man who is blackmailing Casper.

Lazarus Winslow.

How he found out that information on Casper—information forty years old—no one will probably ever know. But if that's what he had on Casper, then he'd love what he could find on me. With the older furniture maker gone, Winslow's attentions may turn to another way to earn the money lost by being down a man in the workshop. A shame Casper didn't name his accuser. I don't want Winslow to turn his attention to me.

One of my secrets...I didn't do the deed, but Mr. Jack might feel obliged to ditch me anyway. My only consolation, if it comes to that, will be to tell the boss what happened before the accountant can. Not my only secret and not the most important one, but the one that's gonna hurt the worse.

Like the ghost of that Captain Lafitte, I need to be invisible from now on.

———

Luck abandons me one evening when I wind up being in the parlor putting the checkers away after all the others leave for the night—but for Lazarus Winslow.

He proceeds to pull up a chair next to me, capturing me in the corner by the checker table. "You've wheedled your way into this home and family, haven't you? You think you're pretty smart, don't you? You can always disappear, you know?" His nasty questions came one after the other. For such a pleasant looking man, he has a disposition like a snake. Silent and deadly.

"What do you want, Winslow?" I don't push back into the cushion of the chair, though the man sits far too close. Air seems lacking.

"Want? For you to leave." He lifts his hand and studies his nails as if this was the most innocent of conversations instead of one of the strangest.

"Why? What have I done to you?" I hiss.

"You've put yourself too high. You belong in the streets." That hand with the polished nails eases my way, aimed at stroking my cheek.

This time I sink back in the chair, hard enough that his hand misses me. "You're disgusting," I tell him. At this moment, I don't care if he makes noises about me or not. I'm not letting him touch me.

"Disgusting? Me?" He holds out both hands to his side as if presenting himself to me. "I think not."

"What's under all that pretty vest and fancy pants and shoes is rotten." This time I make no pretense of being nice. Whether he tries to find dirt on me or not, I can't stay in this corner one more minute.

With both hands out, I rise up and push him back into his chair. Like passing a plague victim, I ease by him as fast as possible, standing on tiptoes and sucking in my belly to avoid touching any part of him any more than I already have.

"You won't mention this, you know," Winslow settles back in his chair, one arm laid delicately over his crossed legs. "Jack and his wife would believe me before you. I mean, look at me. A man of means and refinement. And you," he waves a hand in my direction, "A boy from the gutter." His snort of disgust frightens me.

My feet can't move fast enough. I'm a dead man if he gets hold of me.

Once inside my room with the door locked—for the first time since I arrived—I flop on to the pretty blue quilt, letting my breathing slow down.

He doesn't like me. He's a manipulator who takes money in order to keep secrets. He's going after me next. And there's nothing I can do to stop him.

———

Not only is the summer hotter than any I can remember, but the tension in the furniture workshop rises almost as much as the heat each day. I walk on tenterhooks, hoping to avoid Winslow like a lot of the other men. Does Winslow have dirt on all of them? How can Mr. Jack be so blind as to what's happening?

In his defense, he has no reason to worry about anyone blackmailing his employees. Everyone acts like the world is good. Me included.

"Ms. Christie, when's this heat gonna break?" I ask one evening when I return from helping Thomas deliver a wagon full of furniture.

"Mattie and I walked the beach this afternoon, Jonathan. I can't say if the heat will break for good any time soon, but I think...I feel...it seems like..." She put off saying whatever is on her mind.

"Go on. What do you think? You beat Mr. Cline and the weather guys often enough," I say, trying to badger her into a good mood.

"Get on with you." She grins as she dumps an armload of can goods onto the table in the utility room.

"So when's this heat breaking?" I ask again.

"A bit of a summer storm around the 4th I think. Might dampen the celebration considerable."

"That's fine by me if we can dance in the rain."

Sure enough, rain falls but on the third. The 4th of July dawns bright with air so thick I feel like I'm wearing a wet wool blanket instead of a brand new black and white stripped bathing suit Mr. Jack gives me. The family goes to the beach so much we all wear out our bathing costumes right quick. I notice that Juliet looks right pretty in her suit with the soft pink skirt on it, her shapely stocking legs and bare feet. I notice, too, that Ms. Christie's back to her skinny self after birthing Mattie. The woman never stops moving. The more worrisome thing I notice, though, is how frail Lawrence looks these days. Wasting away like. Everyone's tender with him like he's fragile glass. No one mentions how he looks, so maybe it's just my imagination.

The only bug in the butter churn this whole year so far is Winslow. Since Casper left and he cornered me in the parlor, he's ignored me. That ain't good, is it? Or is it? I get bumfuzzled about the whole thing now and then. But if he can find dirt on Casper that's forty years old, then he can find something on me. Maybe this silence is his time for digging. Cold fingers tap down my back and leave me shivering.

"Cold, dear?" Ms. Christie tosses a towel my way. I just came out of the water, and I suppose that's as good as any reason for the shakes. Certainly has nothing to do with that dandified snake, Lazarus Winslow.

Late that night, safe in my bed, with the family close and summer's heat retreating a little, I keep telling myself that lie. Shivers have nothing to do with what that accountant might be doing when it comes to me.

———

Mr. Jack has to hire two men by the end of July. One to take Casper's place and one to take Jackson Warner's place. Jackson is a furniture finisher, rubs those pieces with special clothes until they shine. He's a master at what he does. He's been teaching me how to use the smaller tools that smooth out edges as well as the clothes that give each piece such a glow. With his full red beard and the flat cap he wears constantly even in the workshop, even in summer, he's the quietest man I've ever met. Rivals Lawrence in silence at times.

One morning he doesn't show up for work. Mr. Jack notes that and waits to see if anyone contacts him, saying Jackson is ill or hurt. But by evening when no word comes and no Jackson, Mr. Jack comes into the house with worry riding him.

"Not like the man. Most punctual man I've ever met. Gets to the shop when it opens and stays to the last minute. Never leaves. Heads straight for his room when he's done. I've never heard him say a thing about family or evenings out or anything. Something of a hermit."

"He'll turn up, dear," Ms. Christie tells him as she sits with the baby.

Jackson Warner doesn't show up for three days. But he does the fourth. On the far west end of the island, some men dropped the anchor of their fishing boat. When they pulled up that same anchor hours later, Jackson's body comes with it.

No one recognized him, so his body went to the police morgue.

Mr. Jack and I head to the police station the fifth morning. "I'd like to report a missing man, officer."

"Come round this way, sir, and let Bronwell here take down the information." We follow the officer to a chair beside a desk. This Bronwell takes out paper and a pen and asks Mr. Jack to describe the man and when he was last seen. The more information and details Mr. Jack gives Bronwell, the slower he writes until he lays the pen down. "Come this way, sir."

We follow him down a hallway, turn left, then right until we walk down a darker hallway, one without windows. "In here, sir." Bronwell lets us go through the double doors first. "Doc, these fellas want to see the body brought in last night."

"Body?" I tug at Mr. Jack's sleeve. "I ain't never seed no dead body before."

"Neither have I, Jonathan. Well, apart from my parents when they died. But I don't think this is quite the same."

A man wearing a full body apron and covers pulled up over his shirtsleeves rolls out one of those medical stretchers on wheels. On top lies something covered by a sheet. I'm not feeling too good about seeing whatever's under that cover. Mr. Jack looks at me, and I give him a swallow. Could this gruesome sight have anything to do with the missing man we came in to report on?

Without ceremony, the man—the doctor I presume—whisks back that sheet. I take one look and head to a large barrel at the side of the room. As I toss my belly of breakfast, Mr. Jack joins me. Not something I ever wanted to do with him—tossing our guts up together.

"Sorry about that, gentlemen," Bronwell says behind us. "I guess I'm used to the sight. Follow me...when you can."

Mr. Jack and I stand but hold the barrel. My legs feel like overcooked noodles. Limp!

The man with the covered shirtsleeves has removed the body and now offers us a small towel apiece. He also offers two glasses of water. We each sip, spit and repeat. Then use the towel to wipe our mouths, all without looking back into what we know now is the police morgue.

Bronwell holds the door open for us once more. We follow him back to his desk where he pulls up a second chair for me.

"I take it that was your missing man, Jackson Warner?"

"Yes, that's him."

Mr. Jack stopped short of saying, "That's what's left of him," but I thought it.

"Turns out his name isn't Warner. It's Velloskos. He's from New York. A Russian who came into America years ago. He killed a man in the part of the city called Brooklyn, then disappeared. We can clear that murder off the books."

"Yes, but what about this murder?" Mr. Jack asks.

"What murder?"

"Wasn't he murdered?"

"Doc says he thinks the man was fishing, slipped, hit his head on rocks, then tumbled into the gulf. We found abandoned fishing gear up the beach a ways along with his pocketbook. Though his name wasn't in there, he had notes about furniture sizes. When you came in, I thought of that body. When you described him, I knew we had our man."

Somehow, I know that man didn't die by accident. Anyone can get hit in the head and it looks like an accident.

Or am I imagining things?

———

Though Jackie heads back to school this morning, Louise and Lawrence stay home. Ms. Christie says they must wait one more year before going to the first year of primary school. How disappointed they look, standing at the front door watching Mr. Jack drive off with the older brother in the family buggy.

Labor Day came and went. The Zimmerman family joined others at the city park bandstand for a day of music and speeches about working men in the unions.

"I fear we've overdone ourselves, dear," Mr. Jack says when he helps the family from the buggy near the back gate. Coming home never felt so good to me.

Ms. Christie steps down, then takes Mattie from me where I still sit in the buggy surrounded by sleeping children. "Thank you, Jonathan. Would you carry Lawrence? The little man is worn out."

"Yes, ma'am."

Upstairs I help Lawrence get to bed, while Mr. Jack takes Jackie in hand. Ms. Christie takes care of Louise, while Mattie sits on her sister's bed, holding a toy her maw brought to entertain her. Not long after that I hear Ms. Christie lay Mattie down for the night.

As I close the door to the twins' room, I see Mr. Jack and Ms. Christie in serious discussion. I head for my own room, but Mr. Jack calls me to his side.

"Do me a favor, please?"

"Yes, sir." I figure he wants me to take the buggy and Gerty around to the barn.

"Drive Ms. Christie to the beach. She's uneasy, and maybe this will calm her. I'd go, but she says I bother the feeling of the weather."

"Sorry about that, sir." I can't imagine this lady telling her husband— a man she loves more than life if I'm any judge—that he messes up her feel for the weather.

"Take care of her, son." He pats me on the arm, kisses his wife and tells her, "I'll wait in the parlor for you."

"Thank you for understanding, my dear. This weather...something's wrong. I need to see..."

"I understand, sweetheart. Go with Jonathan, and do whatever it is you need to do, but hurry home to me."

"Aw, Jack, I love you so much." They cuddle for a minute, forgetting I'm anywhere around.

Eventually they turn loose, and both go down the stairs. I come behind, then follow Ms. Christie out on to the porch, while Mr. Jack turns right into the parlor.

"You know what I'm talking about, Jonathan. I have to feel the weather." She looks so earnest, almost apologetic.

"I know, ma'am." I lead her to the buggy, and we drive to the beach, several blocks south of the house.

"Wait here," she says without looking at me. I promised never to smoke in the house or around the children. But I'm in need of a smoke now. Out comes my last one and a fire stick. Striking it, I pull in deep breaths of smoke, while I watch Ms. Christie.

Alone she walks to the water's edge. Hand out, turning this way and that. Head up, eyes closed. Head tilted first one way, then another. She squats and lets a wave wash over her hand. She does this several times.

I have to admit she's unnerving me. This time the weather thing seems more serious. Almost dark, sinister. Evil. I feel it like she must. I don't feel the changing weather like she does. But I get a sense of danger just from watching her.

She returns, casting glances over her shoulder, back toward the horizon. She fills me with dread when she stops by the buggy where I sit. Quickly I put out the smoke against the front of the buggy and toss the butt onto wet sand.

"Have you ever read anything by a writer named Shakespeare, Jonathan?" She doesn't look at me, talks to me but stares out at the black waters of the gulf.

"No, ma'am."

"He wrote a play called *Macbeth*. Macbeth was a king, and he dealt with three witches. They came looking for him to begin with, but then he went looking for them in the end. The phrase 'something wicked this way comes' comes from that play."

We wait—I wait to hear more, and she waits for... I have no idea.

"Something wicked this way comes, Jonathan. And I fear it will be massive."

"What's going to happen to us?" I have to know.

"I don't know. I don't know."

————

"Did you find the weather forecast in the newspaper?"

I jump. Ms. Christie is right behind me, our minds thinking alike this morning.

"Forecast says a gulf storm headed to Florida. Might be some rain this weekend, but that's all." She reaches for the newspaper, and I hand it over willingly. As she scans the forecast I just read to her, I move to the parlor window. Clear skies. How can something massive come out of such hot blue skies?

"Maybe you're wrong this time, ma'am." She's moved up beside me.

"I don't think so, Jonathan. I wish it were so. But there's something wrong in the gulf. That storm...the one the bureau says went to Florida. I can't help but wonder if it really did."

In the distance, I hear a dog bark. A neighbor walks by with her son, not yet three years old. Behind me, I hear Juliet singing as she dusts. Mattie sits in a pen that Mr. Jack made for her. Soft blankets pad the bottom, so she won't hurt herself if she tumbles. She's crawling and sitting up but not yet walking. Above stairs, Lawrence is silent, but I hear Louise talking to him. How can I enjoy such a perfect life with this potential threat hanging over us?

"Best be off to work, sir. Mr. Jack will be wondering where you are. Errands don't usually take this long." She smiles at me, but it's not her usual sunny one. This one is strained. Her eyes keep glancing out the window, watching the metal wind chime as it sways on the front porch.

Her nervousness creeps over into me. On the way back down the block to the workshop, I snag a smoke I kept in my room. When I enter the workshop doors, someone grabs me by the collar and hauls me around the edge of the building into that same alley where I eaves dropped on Casper not long ago.

With a large hand over my mouth, I have no chance to call out for help. Slammed up against the wall, I fight for breath as I shake my head to clear my vision.

Winslow!

"What in damnation are you doing?" I demand, attempting to loose myself from his grip.

"Quiet, boy. And listen to a proposition." Winslow still has his arm across my chest, the pressure of his body pinning me to the wall. He's got such a wickedly pleased look to him that I immediately realize he's dug up that one thing I wanted to remain buried.

"You listening?"

I start to speak, but he claps a big hand back over my mouth.

"Just nod."

One nod is all he gets.

"Isn't it interesting that your old man is a bank robber? Wonder if you two pulled off heists here in Galveston while y'all stayed here? Three banks were robbed in a two-month time span in 1894. Humm, that would have made you about nine? A bit young but then you might have been holding the reins on the buggy outside each bank. Two men inside. Who's to say you weren't a third one like a few witnesses saw?" He chuckled, obviously delighted with his find.

"Now what can I get out of you that will make me stay quiet?"

To my disgust, he rubs against me. Low-like.

"Ah, I see you understand my demands. You don't make much money, so blackmailing you for your paycheck won't get me anything. But you're a pretty one—all tall, smooth brown hair and those green eyes. That sweet mouth."

Now I'm getting sick behind his hand. I start squirming but realize he's taking too much pleasure from that, so I start gagging. Only the fake gagging turns real as soon as he moves his hand away. I throw up the pancakes Vassy made for our breakfast. Some of the puke splatters on his shoes.

Quick as a wink, his hand is back but this time around my throat. "I'd not try that again, boy. Listen to the deal. Break the deal and you'll not only be tossed out of the Zimmerman's cozy home and Mr. Jack's workshop but you'll probably wind up in jail. At least I'll make sure you do. Understand?"

As near as I can with his hand tucked firmly under my chin pressing against my windpipe, I nod.

"You'll say nothing to anyone about this. Friday night after work, we'll meet up at a place I know. Just you and me...well, and maybe one or two others. We'll make a night of it. And if you're as good as you look, you might pass on word to the Zimmermans that you're staying with friends for the weekend. By Sunday evening, you'll be too sore to move much, and that will seal our bargain."

"It's not a bargain if I don't show up," I manage to get out.

Mistake! He uses his body and arm against my throat to lift me high enough against the wall that my toes dangle, barely touching the ground.

"You'll show up. Thirty minutes late and I'll return and ask to speak to Mr. Jack in his office at the workshop. Humm, if he gets hot about what I tell him...or tries to defend you...well, it might not go well for him, let's just say."

"You can't hurt Mr. Jack!" I grind out, barely conscious from lack of air as his arm squeezes harder.

Like a pelican diving in on fish, his face swoops close to mine, his breath bathing my face. "I'd not bet on that, young master Jonathan, favorite of the Zimmermans."

He's jealous! And crazy and what's the word for...a disgusting unnatural practice.

Gradually he lowers my body until my feet stand flat again. His arm against my throat pulls away. Like a peacock, he shakes himself out, settling all the ruffles I made in his get-up. He pulls his waistcoat down and uses both hands to smooth back his hair.

"You'll say nothing to anyone. And you'll come to me Friday evening at an address I'll give you at closing time." He starts to walk away but turns to give me a nasty glare. "Tell anyone at your peril. Or..." He walks on but calls back, "Or Mr. Jack's."

———

Courage ain't something I ever thought about. Soldiers and sailors are brave. They have the guts to fight against armed men or go up against waves and weather that would just as soon kill them as not. I threw my guts up in that police morgue when I had to look at what was left of Jackson Warner. I had no courage then.

Somehow Lazarus Winslow found out something I don't want anyone knowing. That lie Mr. Jack asked me about when they wanted me to move in. Well, that's the secret lie, and it ain't pretty. How he found out ain't important. No more important than how he found out about Casper or that Jackson Warner. Casper up and left. Winslow could probably find him if he wanted to, but I suspect he wants to bother folks nearby, so he can keep tabs on them. Jackson probably didn't pay his blackmail dues or maybe even threatened to tell the police. All he got was dead.

I might die, but more important, Mr. Jack or maybe Ms. Christie or one of the younguns' might get hurt. That can't happen. But what can I do about it?

I pass on supper tonight. Wasn't easy as Vassy made some German food that smelled mighty tempting. While my stomach wanted to eat, my mind said no. So here I am, pacing my bedroom. Wondering what to do. Wondering if I can give up this family that I've come to love. Wondering if what I could face with Winslow is something I can bear.

"Jonathan?" A soft knock at my door...Ms. Christie. I groan because more than Mr. Jack she's the last person I want to see right now. Not only can she read minds, but she sees right through me most the time.

I want to ignore her, pretend I'm asleep.

But I can't.

She knocks again.

"Coming, ma'am." With a heavy heart, I open the door. She stands in a soft glow of light that they leave on after the children have gone to bed. It's late, later than I realize.

"Mr. Jack and I have listened to you pace for over two hours now. It's time to tell us what's wrong, so we can help you."

I groan again. I want to lie. But one lie won't fix another. Solemn-like I nod. "Yes, ma'am, but my grip is packed...just in case."

"Jonathan?" Shock sets hard on her features as one hand goes up to clutch her throat, like whatever I'm gonna say will make her sick. She may be more right than she knows.

She holds out her hand, something we both know I can't refuse. This time I can't take it. It would be dishonest.

I walk past her, then turn, not knowing where she wants to go. She moves past me, a wounded sad look in her eyes. I've hurt her without even trying.

We go to their sitting room, this side of their bedroom. She points to a chair. Mr. Jack sits across from me, and she sits between us, facing the unlit fireplace.

Neither speaks. I can't. My throat is shut tight with all the words I want to say but just can't. Some of those words would say how much I love them and want to stay. Some of those words would tell them how dishonest I really am.

"Tell us what's bothering you, son." Mr. Jack leans forward in his chair, in his usual studying pose, elbows on knees, hands clasped in front, eyes steady on.

Three swallows it takes to screw up my courage—that courage only soldiers and sailors have. Not kids fifteen years old. But here goes...the question is: where to begin? And in telling them what I must, can I keep my last secret from them? One that isn't so bad, just not quite the truth of the matter as they know it.

With a nod like Ms. Christie might give when her mind's made up, I begin. "Long time ago after Maw died, Paw lost his job. He ups and decides we'll go to Galveston. He's got a friend here, and we can stay with him." So far so good. I breathe a little easier. "Down past the docks are some shanties. That's where we found his friend, Jacob. While I stayed to home, Paw and Jacob went out most every day. I never asked where they went. I didn't ask where they got the vittles or cash they brought in every night. Wasn't a lot but more than Paw and I'd seen in a long time. I heard the two of them hatching some kind of plan one night. Couldn't tell what it was, just that it was mighty secretive.

Next day, Paw tells me I'm to drive a closed buggy. You know, one of those got windows, but they're all closed up most times. Even the driver sits behind the curtain. Keeps the bugs out, Paw said. I can't tell you how proud I was, me...driving for Paw and Jacob as they went about their business. When I stopped the buggy by the bank, I never thought about them doing anything bad. 'Keep your eyes open, son,' Paw told me. For what? He never said, and I never thought to ask. Two shots rang out, and Paw and Jacob came pounding outta that bank lickety-split. They dived into that carriage with Paw shouting at me to 'drive, drive!' I whipped that ol' horse a good lick, and we galloped down the street.

'Turn here. Turn there,' Paw shouted at me as I cracked the whip. About a half mile from the bank, Paw shouts for me to pull into an alley up ahead. I swerve that old buggy and almost dash us up against the wall, but I make it. Paw and Jacob bail out, carrying two bags apiece. I could see a big pistol tucked into Paw's belt. I just knew Jacob had one, too.

'What'd you do, Paw?' I shouted as he and Jacob took up lookout spots at the corner of the alley. 'Done got us enough money to last a long time,' Paw said, grinning like a fool. Right then and there, I realized I'd just been part of a bank robbery. I drove the buggy that took them away with all that money they stole. I couldn't stay with them! Bank robbers get kilt or go to prison! While they was looking for the police, I sneaked out the other end of the alley and ran all the way back to Jacob's house. I gathered up what was important and lit out of there. I never saw Paw again, but I heard about him."

After all that, I suck in enough air to rob Mr. Jack and Ms. Christie. I can't look them in the face. That would be more than I can bear, to see the look of disgust and mis-trust.

"What did you hear about your paw?" Mr. Jack asks.

"After I skedaddled, I kept my ear to the ground about those two. They hit another bank but then lit a shuck out of Galveston to Houston. Some of the folks around Jacob's house told me as they cleaned up the place to rent out to some other fella. I kept hanging around until one old lady dragged me aside one day and showed me the newspaper. Two men tried to rob a big bank in Houston, but the police got there fast and shot them dead. The paper said they were Jon Evans, my paw, and Jacob Lightner, that guy we stayed with."

"This is the secret you kept from us? The one you said would only hurt you if we knew?" Ms. Christie asks, her face full of anxiety, her hands for once calm in her lap, though I can see she holds them tightly wound.

"Yes, ma'am." My head can't hang any lower. I'm that ashamed.

"You knew nothing of their plans, Jonathan. You had no idea until they came running out of the bank."

"That's true, sir, but I drove the buggy that helped them get away."

"How old were you then, Jonathan?"

"Eight, I reckon, sir. Maybe nine. Don't remember exactly."

"So, if someone found out, you're thinking you'll go to jail?" Ms. Christie does that mind reading thing again.

"Yes, ma'am. I'm sorry I kept that from you. I didn't mean no harm. I'd never hurt you or Mr. Jack or any of the children. I'm sorry," I repeat as tears roll down and splat on my hands. On fingers clinched so tight, the tears sit like diamonds in the glimmer of the electric lights around us.

"All right, Jonathan, let's set that aside for a moment," Mr. Jack says.

My chest rests easier just knowing he's not kicked me out the door yet.

"This secret's been around a long time. That's not what's got you pacing and fuming, worried half to death if I read your face right."

Oh God, he's gonna ask, and I'm gonna tell about Winslow.

"Tell us what's got you so riled up. We can help," he adds.

"I'm not sure anyone can, sir."

"Try us." He winks. Ms. Christie gives a decided nod. For me, that's a sure sign of hope.

"Well, sir, ma'am. Someone found out about Paw and got hold of me, threatening-like."

"What does this person want? Can we go to the police?"

Now that we're discussing this, I'm not sure I can say what Winslow wants me to do. It's against nature.

"Come on, son. You've started. Might as well finish, so we can clean up this mess and get on living our lives in peace."

How I hope we can.

"This man...he found out and cornered me. He don't want money. He knows I don't make hardly any, being just a kid and a helper and not a regular working fella. But he thinks I'm..." I gulp and spit out the word. "Pretty." My face heats up something fierce as they gape.

"Well, I never!" Ms. Christie says, patting her cheek and fanning herself.

"Bastard!" Mr. Jack says as he pounds the arm of his chair. "He wants to spend time with you, doesn't he?" It's not a question though. He knows what happens when a man wants a man or a boy in this case.

I nod, too sick to speak.

"What if you don't show up?"

"He'll hurt folks I love."

"Well!" Ms. Christie jumps up and swallows me in a hard embrace. "He can't do that!"

"Yes, ma'am, he can. He's a snake in the Garden of Eden, if you catch my drift."

"We know him?" Mr. Jack's mind must be whirling round and round, thinking of all the folks he knows.

"Yes, sir. Right handily you do."

"Someone in the boarding house?"

My nod confirms his guess. I'm not about to speak the name. But these folks ain't stupid. A bit of thinking and they'll figure it out.

Now it's Ms. Christie who paces. She's not as familiar with the men who live here. No one is: Fuller minds his store and is a kindly fella when at the house. McGraw and Thrill, the railroad men, are a bit rough but courteous enough to work on the trains without offending the paying riders. Mr. Jones who works at the dock speaks little, his language rough and his manners as well. But he's not a mean man, just one used to bossing and getting the dock work done. That leaves one man, the snake that hides among the kindliness of these folks.

"Lazarus Winslow." Mr. Jack speaks the name so softly that it's not a kindness but a death pronouncement.

"We need proof, Mr. Jack. He's a shifty one. He's not going to walk into any trap," I put out fast, afraid the man will up and strangle Winslow, then go to jail.

"Shifty, you say? Has he done this to anyone else?" Mr. Jack's voice rises, a note of disbelief in his tone.

"Yes, sir. A few of the men. Most of them," I admit. "Winslow holds dirt on them like he found on me. They're afraid to say anything for fear Winslow will do something drastic. Bad enough he docks their pay as punishment."

"He does what?" Mr. Jack's riled now. He jumps up and stomps over to the mantle. "I'll kill him myself!"

"No, you won't, sir!" I grab at him and swing him around. "You'll go to jail or worse. I got a plan. I hadn't meant to include you. I planned on going it alone, but if you help, we might be able to pull the fangs on that son of a bitch." I realize I cussed in front of a lady and immediately apologize. "Sorry, ma'am."

She waves me off. "What's your plan, Jonathan?"

"I've only got 'til Friday night before..." I can't even say what Winslow wants. "This being Tuesday evening, it's too late to do what I want, but we can do it tomorrow night."

"And what's that?" Mr. Jack's listening now, his rage controlled.

"We make like nothing's amiss at work tomorrow. Wednesday after work, we follow Winslow. See where he goes. Who he meets. What he does. If he's like what I think, he won't go too long without meeting up with his..." What do you call the sort of fellas that men like Winslow meet?

"*Lover* is what I heard someone say once in church. That sort of thing goes against the Bible. But it exists anyway. Folks like that hide their activities well. We might not learn anything in one night."

"That's true, sir. Might take a few nights to ferret out where he goes and who he meets," I admit.

"We'll do it! Find that snake's den and catch him before he can hurt you...or anyone else. It's a deal?" Mr. Jack asks not only me but his wife. Makes sense. She's part of our lives. No sense in keeping any more secrets —though I do have one little one left. I'll worry about that one after this weather thing Ms. Christie's worried about.

"Deal, sir!"

He shakes first my hand, then turns to his wife. "Deal, my dear?"

"Of a certain, Mr. Zimmerman," she declares emphatically as she shakes his hand and then mine. "I'll man the home fires and watch for an invasion of snakes, while you two go a'huntin'."

―――――

Wednesday comes, and I'm not sure which to worry about more— Winslow and his plans for me or Ms. Christie who paces more and keeps a constant eye on the window. Going to the porch at all hours. Smelling the air. Holding out her hand to feel the breeze that's picked up.

Mr. Jack sends me on a dozen errands all over Galveston that day. "We have to keep you away from Winslow. He might be able to read your face as well as my wife does. You're not afraid anymore. That would tip him off," he says as he gives me and Thomas a list of things to pick up and five pieces to deliver.

Not afraid? What does Mr. Jack know? I'm terrified...yes? No. Actually, I'm not as scared as I was last night. Maybe them having my back, going along with my plan, has put steel in my backbone. No matter. I'm glad to be out of the workshop that day. Thomas lets me snooze in the back of the wagon unless he needs me. The night's gonna be a long one, and the rest is helpful, though the old man has no idea he's helping with the plan.

———

We follow Winslow for two nights. By late Thursday, we're both worn out and chilled. The wind's out of the north, which is odd for this time of September. Winslow goes to his apartment, then swings out along the street, walking with a cane that makes him look fancy. He's changed clothes, wearing one of those hand-stitched vests with a cloak over his shoulders. Mr. Jack whispers that he looks like a man going to the opera down along the Strand. Thankfully, Winslow never takes a cab. We'd be hard pressed to catch one late at night.

We hit pay dirt after midnight Thursday. Winslow makes his way to a house, lit but with curtains drawn across the windows. While a man stands outside—a guard or watchman, Mr. Jack says—we make our way along alleys until we come up beside the house. An abandoned house stands on one side of this softly glowing house Winslow entered, and a dark home, probably a weekend home, stands on the other, its windows shuttered.

Together we peer in. I don't know about Mr. Jack, but my eyes bug at the sight. Men kissing men. Men half dressed, doing things I only thought a man and wife do. In a dim corner sits a man on the lap of another. A naked man with another naked man. Someone calls out. The man on top turns. Lazarus Winslow! Winslow laughs as if he hasn't a care in the world, then turns back to his fornicating.

I've never seen such in my life and hope I never again. My eyes must be bugging out. I'd have stared at the sights in there until my mind melted, but Mr. Jack slaps a hand over my mouth to keep me quiet, then pulls me away from the window. Sweat covers his face despite the wind that's picked up in the last two days. The moon long ago gave way to dark rolling clouds.

"Best we get home and decide what to do about this, son," he whispers near my ear. He jerks his head back toward the end of the alley, indicating we should leave the way we arrived. Neither of us can afford to get caught here. We'd be part of the gulf and fishes soon enough, I reckon, if so. "And we can't tell Ms. Christie what we saw. Not blow by blow."

"Right you are, sir." My mind's still having trouble getting rid of the sights I saw. No need to share that!

————

"We have to call the police. Let them raid the place." Ms. Christie settles the situation.

"Right. I'll go tomorrow, while Jonathan stays here. If Winslow comes around, you can meet him, Jonathan, but, my dear, you'll not leave the two alone. Understood?"

"Yes, sir."

"Yes, dear."

"First thing Friday morning I'll set our plan in action with the police. They can raid the place tomorrow evening and take all those...those... folks to jail."

Mr. Jack leaves after breakfast. Dark heavy clouds fill the sky. Ms. Christie calls me into the parlor shortly after Jackie leaves for school. Fearing Winslow is in there, I drag my heels until she calls me more sharply. "Jonathan, get in here. I need you."

I hustle right on in and find her at the window, the curtains clutched in her hand so tight I know Juliet will have a fit getting the wrinkles out.

"Ma'am?"

"Take me to the beach immediately. Juliet is watching the children. No time to waste." She all but runs toward the back of the house. The weather is unusually warm and close. Clouds race across the sky, while a north wind blows hard enough to billow Ms. Christie's skirts, forcing her to gather them. My cap lifts, and I make a grab for that.

"What's happening?" I ask as I race with her to the barn. Ol' Gerty won't be happy going out into what looks like the beginning of a humdinger of a storm.

"Remember when I talked about that writer?" She helps me harness the horse to the buggy and makes it in before I can even offer her a hand.

"Yes, ma'am. That Shakespeare fella who wrote the play about the king and witches."

"That's the one. Remember what I said about this weather that night?"

I already have the horse headed for the beach. As we roll closer, I see waves mounting higher than I ever remember seeing them.

"Remember?" She calls me back to her question.

"Not exactly, but it wasn't good. That I do remember," I answer over a strong wind snatching my words away.

"Something wicked this way comes." She jumps down from the buggy and races toward the water's edge. Only it's hard to tell where the tide's edge is. One wave rises, then falls with a crash. Smaller waves roll in, one after the other, then what seems only seconds later another huge wave rises up and crashes. The spray sends Ms. Christie back up the beach as she tries to keep her hair out of her face, while holding her shawl firmly around her shoulders.

The wind catches the shawl and sends it out ahead of her, toward the raging waters. She manages to hold one corner though. Like a flag, frantic to get loose, it whips and snaps.

Gradually she backs up step-by-step until she bumps into me. I got down from the buggy right after she did and moved right up behind her, not wanting to bother her, but close enough to grab her if one of those waves caught her in a current.

"Bad?" I ask, as my cap sails off my head and disappears among the waves. The roar of the water and crashing of the big waves makes it almost impossible to be heard.

"Bad!" She points to another wave that rises and falls so hard it makes a deafening noise. "Those are what the weather bureau calls swells. Wind from a storm pushes the water until it comes up against land—like it's doing right now. The more powerful the wind and wave the more powerful the storm."

I watch wave after wave roll in, every third one or so mounting the air, then falling as if trying to pound the sand beneath it. A storm is coming. A big one. A bad one.

"How soon?"

"Soon!"

Scared now, afraid of what's going to happen if a monster storm hits the island, I pull her back to the buggy. Rushing now, I push her in, then run around, grab the ground lines where I tied Gerty and turn the buggy around. Whipping the horse, we race back to the house.

"I have to tell Mr. Jack," I pant as I all but push her into the house.

"He's with the police. I think he plans on staying with them."

"What? And leave me here?" That hurts. "I want to be there!"

"Jonathan!" Ms. Christie grabs me and stops me from racing out. "You're needed here. Jack and the police can do what they must. But we have to get ready for this storm. It's going to be a bad one. Rain, flooding, wind. We need to gather supplies, wrap them up safely and put everything as high in the house as we can. Are you with me?" She grabs my shirtfront. "Are...you...with...me!"

"Yes! Yes, ma'am!" I give up any notion for racing off to join the forces taking down Winslow. The idea that Mr. Jack *is* gone and I'm the only man around jerks me back to reality. "Tell me what to do."

Rain hits the window hard enough to sound like a beam hitting the wood. We both jump.

"The first thing we do is send Juliet and Vassy home. They can't stay here. They need to be with their families."

"Right."

"I'll tell them, and you can drive them home. Be careful. The rain has let loose something fierce. If this is only rain, I'll get down on my knees and thank God every day for the rest of my life," she mutters as she heads upstairs. "Get the buggy and pull it up to the gate. The ladies will be there in a few minutes."

She races up, and I race out.

———

The ride around Galveston to take Vassy and Juliet home turns out to be a test of wills. Gerty wants no part of the storm. Vassy and Juliet both think this is merely a rainmaker, a storm that will wash out the high-sided streets and leave a sweeter cleaner city. They want to stay with the

JANE CARVER

Zimmermans.

I've got my orders. The ladies go home. Final word. No argument. Gerty and I return as soon as we can. Gerty is more than ready to head back to her stable as Juliet dashes inside her home.

On the way, I give thought to Mr. Jack and the men in the workshop. Will this weather force them to leave? Will the plan to catch those unnatural fellas fall through? What about Samuel and his family? And Georgie? Damnation, I wish he were here right now. A little fella like that will be scared even if he has his precious sisters around him.

I pull up to the barn and settle Gerty, but before I return to the house —it's late by now—I have to do one more thing. Winslow expects me at the workshop door at closing time, so he can give me the address where I'm to meet him. I have to show up. Otherwise, he'll get suspicious and screw up the plan the police have.

Rain soaks me good by the time I duck in the small workshop door. Looks like most of the men have moved out early. Might not be a bad idea, considering the rain coming down in buckets.

"There you are, dear boy. I didn't see you all day and wondered if you suddenly came down *ill*." He pouts as he says the word *ill* in a nasty tone.

"I'm here."

He slips a paper into my pocket rather than the hand I hold out. His touch gives me the willies.

"Don't be late. And don't use this weather as an excuse though..." he waggles his brows in a suggestive way, "the rain might be a good excuse to spend the entire weekend with me."

I wait until he leaves before I heave up my lunch.

———

"The children are in bed at last," Ms. Christie says when she meets me in the parlor. Rain lashes the windows like ropes in a high wind. "When will Jack come home?" she worries aloud.

My thoughts, too. The raid will take place any time now. Hopefully he'll get home before night settles in hard and this storm turns uglier.

114

"This is the storm you worried about?" I have to ask.

"Yes, and I fear this is only the beginning."

"The weather report made this sound pretty normal," I have to add that and see what she says.

"Jenny Dine down the street told me early this afternoon that she saw Mr. Cline on the beach. Looked like he was watching the swells. She said he didn't look happy. In fact, she said he scared her to death, his face so full of worry. She was headed home when I saw her. Said she was going to prepare for a bad one, too."

"What can we do? I can't stand here and worry for hours," I admit.

"Me either. Let's get things gathered and up into the attic."

"You think the water will get that high?"

"I hope not, but best be ready if it does. Did you get the ax like I asked?" She walks into the big room at the back of the house.

"Yes, ma'am. What's it for?"

"You ever noticed those round spots in the corners on the first floor?"

"Yeah. Never gave 'em much thought."

"If the water starts rising, we'll knock those plugs out with an ax. Let the water come in. Open the doors if we have to. Just so the water has nothing solid to push against. That way the house isn't knocked off its foundation." She gathers wicker baskets that Juliet uses to carry sheets while telling me.

"You mean the house might...float away?"

"Oh, Jonathan, I was here in '86 when a bad storm came through. Didn't mess with us so much as Indianola, but we knocked out those plugs, and water came up through them. Water ran through the streets, but no one was hurt and no bad damage but to some places along the beach. I've seen what water can do."

Her words scare me. Terrify me even. I've never been where I can't control what's happening, even with help, like this thing with Winslow and Mr. Jack helping. Wind and water ain't nothing you can fight against. Just get ready.

"You gonna help or stand there stiff as a board?" Ms. Christie asks as she hauls out some oiled tarps. Her words are mean sounding, but I know she's trying to get my mind off what's coming.

"Help me line these baskets."

Together we sink the tarps into three baskets, fitting them against the sides so we can fill the baskets with things Ms. Christie thinks we need.

"Take these jugs. Fill them with water and carry them up to the attic. Set them around one of the center floor beams and lash them tight together so they won't roll over and bust. We may need them for a few days if the gulf takes over the water pipes."

Over the next hour, I fill and haul up six big jugs of water. I follow instruction, using rope to tie the jugs firm to a post. Then I head back to the big room. "What's to do next?"

She already has two baskets filled with canned goods, candles and fire sticks. "Help me carry these up. They're too heavy and bulky for one person to carry alone."

We struggle up two flights of stairs. Bumping into the wall now and then, stopping to listen in case we wake the children. Once in the attic, we stop to catch our breath.

"We tie these up too, ma'am?"

"Yes, otherwise the water will wash them right out the window. They'll float like a boat."

Several more hours pass as we fill and haul up two more baskets.

"I thought one more basket would do, but we need blankets and clothes. Who knows what else we might need," she says just as she gives out and collapses on the parlor chair, her head in her hands, sobbing.

"I'm afraid, Jonathan. The storm. Mr. Jack. What's going to happen to us?"

Courage and strength are what I think of when I think of this woman. Not this sobbing hopeless wreck.

"We gotta think the best, ma'am. Hope for the best. We'll be strong folks if we survive all the messes that come our way," I say as I kneel beside her and hold her shaking form.

Eventually her crying stops. "You're right, sir. Perfectly right. But I want to make sure the Lord's not forgotten us. Grab Granny

Zimmerman's two quilts, while I get the family Bible. I think there's one more tarp left to wrap them in." Like a soldier knocked down who struggles to rise again, she pats me on the shoulder, then hustles to the stairs, taking them two at a time, her skirt tucked up above her knees as she runs. I struggle to gather the two huge quilts that sit on a box in the corner. A box filled with keepsakes of her family and Mr. Jack's. She showed me once when she opened it. With no time that day to take out things and show them all to me, she promised to do so someday.

At this moment, I fear that day may never come.

Struggling up the stairs again, we meet at the attic.

"I forgot the tarp!" she says and races away, leaving me alone with nothing but pounding rain and howling wind.

I sit down hard, the quilts piled in my lap. What if the worst happens and the storm washes a bunch of the island away? Never would I have thought something like that possible, but then I've never been in a big storm. And I'm afraid to ask Ms. Christie if that's even possible.

"Jonathan! Jonathan!" At first, I think I'm imagining someone calling my name, not in a loud yell but softly. This time not one pair of feet run up the stairs, but...two? Is Mr. Jack...?

"Jonathan! Look who's home!" Ms. Christie comes through the door first but right behind her comes...

"Mr. Jack!" I jump up, almost stumble over the pile of quilts and throw myself into the man's dripping arms! "You're alive!" His arms envelop me in such a sense of safety that my heart fairly sings.

"Of course I'm alive, dear boy." He pulls Ms. Christie into his embrace as well.

"What happened? Did the police get Winslow? Did you have trouble getting home?"

Ms. Christie and I pepper him with questions.

"Let me change, and I'll tell you both."

We follow him to their sitting room where I wait, while Ms. Christie helps him out of the soaked clothes.

"The wind's still out of the north," he announces when they reenter the sitting room.

"But the waves, Jack. They're so high!" Ms. Christie frowns, studies her shoes, then asks us both, "Do you think the wind's holding back those waves?" Fear etches her words into hard sounds.

"What? You think the waves will be worse if it's a typical storm with the wind coming out of the south?"

"Yes," she whispers.

"Then that would mean..."

"When the wind shifts—if it shifts—the gulf will rise right over the island," she pronounces a death knell for this place.

My mind goes blank. I can't even ask about the police raid. What will it matter if we're all dead? I try to talk, but all I hear is babble. Meaningless words, failed questions.

Suddenly one thing does come to mind—clear as glass on a sunny day. Georgie!

"I gotta go!" I jump up and head for the door.

Quick as a wink, Mr. Jack's there, his back against the door, holding me. I struggle like a mad man.

"I gotta go. Get Georgie!" I can see him in my mind. Rolled and washed away by the gulf that finds him, out there on the dunes alone.

"You can't leave now! It's not safe! Waters already running high in the streets. The current will wash you away!"

Mr. Jack's talking, but I'm not listening.

"Georgie!" I cry out again.

"Your friend will be safe with the sisters," Ms. Christie says, her arms around me from the back, holding me like a mother would a distressed child. "He'll be safe."

"No, he won't. That place. What if the storm washes some of it away? Or does worse. I gotta go get him...bring him here...where it's safe." I fight, but together they're stronger than I am. Mr. Jack finally wrestles me down to the floor and holds me. This time not to prevent me from running out in the storm. But to hold me as I cry.

"I gotta get Georgie!" I wail.

"You can't, son. He's your friend, I know, but—"

"He's not my friend! He's my *brother*! I gotta get him! I kept it a secret," I scream. Once more, I try to rise and run.

But Mr. Jack and Ms. Christie aren't having any of it. They hold me tight.

"I'm so sorry, Jonathan! I'm so sorry, son," Mr. Jack repeats over and over.

"I'm so sorry, my dear," Ms. Christie says as she weeps with me. "But we need you. *I* need you, Jonny," she whispers. "Stay with us...with me."

No one's called me Jonny since my maw died.

"I'll ask God to watch over him, but that's all we can do. The storm's got us," Ms. Christie says. "As soon as we can, we'll bring Georgie home."

My heart broken, my spirit weak, I give up the struggle to leave.

We can do nothing. The fury of wind and rain have sealed our fate. The sun will shine on calm gulf waters again. But will it be soon enough?

———

In the early hours of Saturday morning, the storm is bad enough that we don't dare venture out the door. Mr. Jack keeps the ax handy as together we wait for sunup. Or whatever will pass for sunup on this day. In the past half hour, we've heard the sound of creaking and things banging against the house. A crash somewhere close indicates a building went down. Only with morning light can we gage whether we're going to be safe and merely ride out a bad storm or prepare for worse to come.

I resign myself to the fact that I can't save Georgie by bringing him to the boarding house. I can only pray that he's safe.

Ms. Christie reads my mind. She pulls me against her and reaches for Mr. Jack's hand. "The Lord needs to know our troubles, son." She bows her head and sends up a prayer that I hope God can hear through all the noise. "Dear Heavenly Father, we ask you to protect us and those we love. Juliet, Vassy, Samuel, our neighbors and the workers at the shop. We beseech you to hold Your hand over those at the orphan asylum, protect those little ones. And if it's Your will, please protect our Georgie. Bring him safely to us. Give us courage to face tomorrow, Lord, for we are afraid. Something bigger than us comes, and we can't defeat it. We can only persevere." She takes a sudden breath, as if hit with an idea but calms immediately and finishes. "We ask for strength and Your loving hand to carry us through the day. Amen."

I repeat that even as Mr. Jack does.

Immediately she goes to the box in the corner. "I might not have thought of this on my own, but the Lord put it in my head while I was praying." She opens it and pulls out a small Bible, frayed at the edges, the cover thin, with the paper showing through where leather has worn. "Paul wrote letters to churches. One of them is in Romans." She thumbs the pages carefully, aware as we are of the book's age. "Ah, here." She uses a finger to keep her place as she reads aloud, "From Romans 5, Paul wrote here in Grandpa Zimmerman's King James Bible. 'But we glory in tribulations also: knowing that tribulation worketh patience. And patience, experience; and experience, hope. And hope maketh not ashamed."

"I got no idea what that means, ma'am," I admit.

"Jonathan, Paul told those early Christians that tribulations—bad times—brings about perseverance—staying power. That staying power brings about character—the way you're made...all those things inside you that makes you *you*!" She's rolling now, explaining what this Paul fella wrote about. "All those things in you—that character—brings about hope. And," she fairly glows as she finishes, "Hope does not disappoint!"

I must still look confused.

"In other words, dear boy, bad times are coming, and we can stay the course, letting all the good things that make us rise up and hope for the best. If we hope, things will work out."

I roll my eyes. I've not had much to do with the Bible, but I do believe there's something bigger than me moving me along through life. If that something—the Lord, I suppose—says we stay and make the best of what happens, then I'm thinking Georgie will be all right—somehow. Maybe he'll survive this, and maybe he won't. By now, it's outta my hands.

"Jack, now that we've asked the Lord to watch over us and those we love and care for..." She looks around as if seeing her home for the last time. "Now that we're prepared as best we can be...tell us what happened with the police tonight."

In my despair about Georgie and such, I plumb forgot about the police raid. Hours ago, that was a big thing. Now it doesn't feel like such a big deal.

"We staked out the house where Winslow went the other night. I told the police that with the weather getting bad and the weekend coming up, the man would probably hole up there until the storm passed. They agreed. Oh, and by the way, Jonathan, those friends of yours—Rowdy and Jason—they did call the police and tell them about the man who hired them and the fire at Mrs. Abbey's place. The sergeant said he could hear a train whistle in the background, so I figure they took your advice. Called before hopping a train north. I'm not sure there's anything the police can do about that fella now or not, but at least the boys told what happened."

"Glad to know they're not all bad."

Above stairs, I hear the sounds of someone up—probably Jackie. "Quick, sir, before the children come down. What happened tonight?"

"As soon as Winslow entered, we waited ten minutes, so everyone would be settled inside. Then the police blocked off each entryway and watched the windows in case anyone tried to jump out. Someone inside had a gun and shooting broke out. By the time things calmed down, they arrested a dozen men and called for a morgue wagon to pick up three dead men. One of them was the one we saw with Winslow, Jonathan. I heard Winslow call out, scream when a shot hit the fella. He wrestled with one of the policemen and hit him hard enough that he escaped out the back door."

"Winslow escaped? That's not good, Mr. Jack. What if he comes for you?" I have a sudden fear that the weather's not all we have to worry about.

"I'm not too worried. Several policemen did call me by name, asking me if this fella or that one was the one I was looking for, but I think Winslow left before that."

"You *think*?" Ms. Christie isn't happy to hear that Lazarus Winslow might know who led the raid. "Jack, what if he comes looking for you? We could be in danger." She's back to wringing her hands.

As if anyone is moving around in weather like this? As if one man looking for another this day will happen.

"It's going to be all right, my dear." Mr. Jack takes her into his arms just as a wail breaks out above stairs. "Sounds like the baby needs you." He kisses the top her forehead and gives her a little push. That and the baby calling for 'Mama' send her on her way.

"Things are bad, aren't they, Mr. Jack? Winslow will seek revenge, whether today or some day in the future."

"Yes, Jonathan. Things are bad. This storm is as bad as any I've seen. The wind could be holding back those waves. If that changes, then this island could wash away."

That grim thought almost makes me forget the other *bad* part. "And if we persevere as Ms. Christie says, then Lazarus Winslow could be looking for you. You'll be watching over your shoulder until he shows up."

"Not if we get him first though. Once this storm clears, the police will be hunting him."

That's a relief! "The sooner they find him the better, if you ask me."

"Agreed. Now let's get those lazy fellas up, so we can see what's in the big room to eat."

———

We dress the children in several layers of clothes, in order to pad them against bumping around if the water rises high enough. Against the chill of wind and water together. Ms. Christie dons a pair of Mr. Jack's denim pants along with her boots, a heavy blouse and a jacket.

"What about tying the children to you with a rope, dear, in case the water washes high enough to carry you out of the house?"

She shakes her head and reasons, "If I get caught by something, then the children have no way to get above the water to safety. They'll be held down by my weight."

This kind of crazy talk leaves me speechless. They're seriously talking about the possibility of drowning? All I can see is that orphan asylum and all those little kids. And Georgie, my little brother. The one I protected when Paw would get mad and stomp around hitting at things... like Maw. That baby came early 'cause Paw got mad at Maw and bashed her so hard she fell. I protected Georgie when Paw up and moved us to Galveston. And I protected my little brother when I realized I helped Paw in a bank robbery. Georgie's the most precious thing I have...all the family I have left. I scooted back to Jacob's house, grabbed food, clothes and that little man and skedaddled.

We never looked back. Somehow that little guy talked his way into a Sister's good graces, not quite telling her the full truth of the matter. That he had a brother. I think over time that nun figured out who I was but knew I had no way to take care of the fella. She and Georgie were thick as thieves most times I saw them. I never felt bad about him being in those big ol' buildings down at the west part of the island.

Now I have to leave him to God's care. Sure as certain, I can't help. The clock on the mantle dings eight times, but you sure can't tell that it's eight o'clock in the morning. Looks like night never left, if you ask my opinion.

Wind rattles the back door. The wind's still blowing from that direction—the north. I pray it stays that way. After what I saw at the beach last night, those rolling mountains of water, I don't want that coming down on me or mine right here in our home. We're blocks from the beach, but Georgie and those orphans are right at the beach.

By now, water's seeping under the door. Rain's hitting the door hard enough to break the glass. The windows bow in now and then with the press of the storm against them. Even as I stand below waiting for Mr. Jack, so we can knock out those floor plugs, the water rises around my ankles. Any minute now, I expect the doors to smash open and water to come rushing in.

Mr. Jack comes down the stair, Jackie right behind him. Ms. Christie follows them slowly, Mattie clutched in her arms, Louise tugging at her jacket.

"We have to hurry, Mr. Jack. Water's coming in fast."

"Right, son. Coming."

The house is dark. The electricity gave out hours ago, and no one's ready to light a candle and have a window break or a door fling open and knock it over. Fire's the last thing we need now even if it is raining buckets outside. I'm already in the parlor and move to join them.

Another noise busts through the storm noise. Sounds like something's bumped hard against the wall.

"What?" Mr. Jack steps down and heads to that big room at the back of the house, the one where I heard the wind hit the door. Only now, the door's standing wide open. The house feels different now that the wind can blow in. I swivel around in time to see the front windows sort of suck in just as the front door not only sucks in but slams back against the wall, the glass shattering. Wind blows straight through now. Water's coming faster. Rising as I watch.

"Get upstairs!" orders Mr. Jack even as he heads for the back door. "Jonathan, see if you can get that front door closed."

Standing in the middle of the house between two open doors, in running water, is a challenge. The wind's pushing me one way while sucking me another. The water's about to knock me off my feet, the current is so fast. Before I can take two steps—hard as that is—I hear, "Winslow!"

I jerk around in time to see Lazarus Winslow in the big room, a gun held up to Mr. Jack. "No!" I yell and race for the back of the house.

Fast as I am, I'm not as fast as the small fella that flashes past me.

"Papa!" Jackie yells as he flings himself at his papa.

A shot rings out. I enter the doorway as Mr. Jack falls, Jackie still clinging to him like a morning glory vine. "Papa!"

Torn, I'm not sure whether to go to the man I've learned to love and see to his wound or go over to the man I've come to despise who's headed out the back door into the storm's fury.

"Jack!" Ms. Christie screams.

She's given the baby to Louise. I see her running for the back room just as a wall of water hits the house, through the front door, moving directly down the hall and out the back door, carrying not only Mr. Jack but Jackie, too! I desperately cling to the heavy oak table that straddles the doorway, giving me a secure place to cling. The water's knocked Ms. Christie off her feet! She's riding the current...headed toward the back door...under the table! I have to get hold of her, or she'll be swept outside!

Timing is crucial. This is happening way too fast. I grab her coat and pray to God it'll hold. All those buttons she did up earlier have to hold! I pull her up, choking on the salt water's she's swallowed. "Ma'am, hold on!" I yell.

The current's not letting up! We have to get upstairs somehow. The children are there.

"We have to get to the stairs. The back stairs. We have to get to Louise, Lawrence and Mattie." My Mattie May—what will become of her if we die here?

"Fight, ma'am! Fight!"

She's fighting all right, but she's fighting me. Trying to reach out into the day's darkness and fury for the man she loves and her oldest child. I fear they're beyond our help. But she's not.

"We have to move. It's too dangerous here." Too late to knock holes in the floor, the house may float off the piers beneath it. My hope is the place doesn't collapse around our ears. "We have to get to the children," I repeat over and over as I push her away from the table and against the wall. The current isn't quite so strong here, away from the direct line between front and back doors. Finally, we make it to the narrow stairs. By now, the water's up to my knees. "We gotta move, ma'am."

Ms. Christie falls into the arms of her children soon enough, and I collapse next to her. "We can't stay here, ma'am. We gotta get higher."

Choked with sobs I can only imagine since the house is now pitch black and the world around us is one big roar, she doesn't speak but reaches out to take my hand. I gather Mattie to me while she takes the twins by their hands, and we climb yet another flight of steps to the attic.

"Where's Papa?" asks Lawrence.

"Where's Jackie," ask Louise.

Where's God in this hell that now passes for Galveston, I want to yell.

How can Ms. Christie explain to her children what just happened? I'm not sure she's even taken it all in yet. While Mr. Jack and his son are gone, I can only pray—the most powerful prayer I can muster up—that Lazarus Winslow's dead and gone to hell. As for Mr. Jack, there's a chance he and his son might survive. If this storm lets up soon.

I cuddle Mattie, knowing that if not for her, Lawrence and Louise, Ms. Christie would have gladly gone out the door on that tide, looking for her husband and son.

I moved a desktop clock up to the attic earlier. Tucked it on top of one of those baskets. While the things inside the baskets, inside the oiled tarps, will be all right, that ol' clock might take on water. But until it does I can pull the glass open and feel the hands. Tell the time. Pass what's left of this day and hope we survive to see the sun again.

"Jonathan?" Ms. Christie holds the twins so close to her that they practically sit in her lap. I still hug Mattie. The children, even baby Mattie, sense the danger that now surrounds us. "What happened? Is he gone? Jackie?"

Did what happen break her spirit? Crush that steel that she has for a backbone? Time alone will tell. In the dark, I can't.

"I heard a bang. Like a door flung open. When I went to check it, Mr. Jack got there first. Jackie came running around me. Winslow was there, with a gun. It all happened so fast, ma'am," I moan. "I couldn't save them. Winslow fired. Mr. Jack fell, and Jackie fell on top of him—"

"Was Jackie shot!" Her gasp of horror rings out above the noise.

"No, ma'am. No! But Mr. Jack was. I tried to get to him but really wanted to go after Winslow. Kill him with my bare hands." I relive those seconds. The smell of salt and gun smoke as gulf water pushed me into that room. The chill where the wind hit my face and hands. The eerie screech of wind as if it were cutting around corners like a knife. So very real. So very horrible.

"Before I could reach any of them, I heard you coming and that wave right on top of you. Mr. Jack—well, he washed right out the back door.

Jackie with him. Winslow had already escaped. I don't know if any of them survived that sweep of water," I tell her frankly. "But—"

"We have to keep the children safe!" She suddenly comes alive.

"My same thinking, ma'am. What do you want me to do?"

"There's some old curtain material up here. Over here in this box. Help me get it out." Like a whirlwind now, she's up and moving, the twins clinging to her as close as possible without getting in her way. She tears open a box and starts pulling out lengths of soft material. I can feel it even as she lays yards of it by me.

"We're safe for now, I think, but you may need your hands to help me hold the children. I refuse to tie the twins to me, but you and Mattie are different. These two might survive without us."

Another grim thing to say.

"But Mattie won't last if you go down. Here, help me." She begins to wind material around me, making a sling that snugs the baby right up next to my chest, her face just below my chin. Standing behind me, she somehow secures the whole tangle without making a ferocious knot in the middle of my back.

"Now...let go," she orders.

Reluctantly I release my hands. The baby doesn't move one inch. She's secure, and my hands are free.

"Good job, ma'am."

"As long as you've got your hands free, you can manage to save both of you," she shouts at me.

The house takes a sudden pitch, rocks as if floating. The sounds change around us.

"Listen!" Ms. Christie grabs my arm for support. She's got hold of Lawrence. I take Louise by the hand.

"What's that noise, ma'am?"

"The wind's changed. Out of the south now. Water'll be coming fast and high now."

"Like it wasn't before?" I ask in disbelief. "This hell can get worse?"

"All that north wind kept the water back. Now there's nothing to stop it."

Things begin hitting the house. Hard enough to bust through. We hunker down next to the center beam that runs up through the house. Shingles from the roof rip off; I can hear them pop, then scratch their way into the wind. Everything loose out there is now flying along with the wind, like bullets from a gun. What once was carried out into the gulf by the north wind is now returning with a vengeance. Nothing can stop what's happening now as this storm tears the island apart.

With the wind change, the house begins to sway. Rocks as if on water. Someone screams. Me? Ms. Christie? Both of us? All of us, including the children? We scream more than once as time goes by. The house sways and tilts. I can't detect if we actually float, but I reason that anything smaller than this big ol' boarding house is now part of so much debris. A window on the south side of the house gives way, and wind tears through like a racehorse outta the gate. We huddle against the north wall now. Bunched up in a tight ball.

Hell can't be this noisy. God can't be so quiet. In that space of time, we hug each other, feeling each pitch of the house and thudding of debris. And I pray. I pray like never before. For me, Ms. Christie and the younguns. Mr. Jack and his son. Georgie and all the others that I care for —Samuel, Juliet and Vassy. While wind whistles through that south attic window, Ms. Christie leans close. "What if something blows through there? Will we be safe, you think?"

"We have to hope so, ma'am." That's all the reassurance I can give her.

Without warning, something does slam into the window, but it's big enough to cover the hole left when the glass and frame gave way. Like a boxer punching his opponent, I can tell more and more debris wedges up against that part of the house. I worry that water will pour right over all that mess and dump right down on top of us.

"Maybe we should move away from this window and more into the middle of the room, ma'am. That stuff over the window may be shutting off the wind, but it may send water pouring over that part of the house. We might get prepared to have that wall collapse and us dumped into the gulf."

If I scare her, that's all right. She must be numb by now, slow to react. I can't afford to be slow.

Giving me one of her decisive nods, we move back to the middle of the room, by the jugs of water and baskets of supplies. I can't help but think that those might be what keeps us alive when this is over. Surely few things smaller than this house will still be standing or be too damaged to use. Things like Vassy's kitchen. Then again, I hope that the damage isn't as bad as my imagination.

In the howling weird sounds, my thoughts turn to those friends. Georgie I've assigned to God's hands. But what about Juliet, Vassy, Samuel and their families? They all live on the east end of the island that is even lower than Avenue L where the boarding house stands.

Ms. Christie unwraps the quilt from around the twins, checking by feel that they're still doing all right. "Jonathan?" she calls. "Come feel Lawrence. Tell me what you think."

Moving to her side, I run my hand under the quilt and rest it against the little man's forehead. "He's chilled, but then we all are. That wind blew lots of spray in." I move my hand down his body, stopping over his heart. Odd...I can't find much of a thump there. My hand moves up to his throat, just like Maw used to do if we were sick.

"He's not breathing so good, Ms. Christie. He's cold, and his heart ain't thumping like a body's would in this storm. I think he's sick."

To my surprise, she begins crying again, softly so as not to wake Louise. The poor little girl's worn out and just naturally dropped off to sleep some time ago.

"Why're you crying, ma'am? Is Lawrence going to be all right?" I rub Mattie's back, seeking comfort. She, too, is asleep.

Ms. Christie reaches for my hand, while holding Lawrence closer, him still wrapped in that quilt. In the middle of a storm that may kill us all, a storm that I hope we all survive, she tells me something I didn't want to know.

"Lawrence was born with a bad heart, the doctor said, after he recovered from a case of scarlet fever when he was a baby. According to the doctor, his surviving was a miracle. But the doctor warned us that our little boy's heart was weak and wouldn't get stronger. He'd not live to see the end of school years."

"Lawrence...is dying?" Besides Georgie, this little man is dearest to my heart. Well, Mattie is my very heart, but Lawrence... He's so small, so fragile. And now I know why.

"This excitement isn't good for him, is it?"

I don't need to see her to know she shakes her head. The idea that this precious little boy might die soon tears me up. The wet that covers my face now isn't from the storm.

"Pray that he makes it through this storm and we can fill his life with joy before..." She can't finish.

"Yes, ma'am. I'm praying. I've been praying ever since this storm began."

She pats my hand and offers encouragement. "Good boy."

With Louise cuddled next to her and Lawrence on her lap, I sit on her other side, shoulder to shoulder with the bravest person I've ever met. If the waves take us tonight, I can say I went with the best of 'em.

Fear and exhaustion take over despite what's happening around us. The house rocking. Debris hitting everywhere, flying through the air like arrows, I'm sure. Waves washing over and through the house. Crashing sounds that scare me to death. A body can only take so much before it gives in to rest. I think we all must have drifted off despite the horror.

———

Silence wakes me. That's an odd thing to realize.

No longer does the wind howl. No longer do things hit the house. No longer does it rock as if floating in gulf waters.

Even the rain has stopped. What do I see through the ragged gash that used to be a north attic window? Brightness. Has someone come with a lantern to find us?

I'll be damned! It's sunshine. The storm's over! We're alive! I want to jump up and dance around the room with Miss Mattie who's rustling around, trying to wake to a morning that should be like any other but probably isn't. Ms. Christie sits beside me, her head on my shoulder, asleep like the twins.

The twins...Lawrence! I carefully lift the quilt away and study his face, watching the side of his neck where the heart beat shows. His chest rises but so slowly that I fear it won't happen. He lives yet. Now that the storm's terror is past, we can take good care of him. Make his life good.

At least I tell myself that.

"Ms. Christie. Ma'am? Wake up. It's over. The sun's out." I bump her with my elbow gently. "Wake up, ma'am."

When I can tell she's awake enough for me to move without her falling over, I get up but do so carefully. I'm not sure how stable the house is. It could crash down on us at any minute maybe.

Ms. Christie hasn't gotten up yet, but she's awake, like I did, staring out the window at the bright light. "Is that the sun?" she asks, a silly question in normal times, but then last night wasn't normal.

"Yes, ma'am. Nary a breeze or raindrop. Just sunshine. Let me check out things below before you disturb Lawrence." Louise is awake but all big-eyed, clutching her maw's arm. "Best I leave Mattie with you. Let Louise hold her. She's wet by the way, and it ain't from the storm," I add. "She's kind of smelly, too, if you know what I mean." I kneel so Ms. Christie can undo the material holding the baby to me. She's only got one hand, what with her holding Lawrence, so getting loose takes a long time. Eventually Mattie slips out of the material into my arms.

"How you doing, little girl?" I snuggle her and watch her grin. She alone will come through this storm with few memories. For the rest of us, our lives will be filled with what happened here in the last twenty-four hours. As Mattie giggles and wiggles, I ease her down on to Louise's lap. "Stay with sister." I catch Louise's glance. "You have to hold her. She can't go running around. We don't know what's safe or what's not." The girl nods, but honestly, I'm not sure how much she understands. Safe? Playing? Will they ever be safe to play again, I suspect she's wondering.

"I'll be back as soon as I can. Stay here...all of you."

I step gingerly to the attic door...what's left of it. The wind through the doors downstairs and the broken attic windows busted this one out hours ago. On the second floor, things aren't as bad as I imagined. The floor slants which tells me the house sits at a tilt, but whether it's safe to stay in I won't know until I can get outside. The windows along the south part of the house, the front facing the beach, are boarded up with debris, looks like. But there's still light from the north kitchen door. Over the banister I see light coming up the hall—strong light. At least I'll be able to get out. Carefully I make my way through the family's rooms. What a mess! The wind tore through shattered windows, and the rain flooded in. At least I think it was the rain. Things on this floor like clothes, quilts, toys and books are tossed around and wet through and through.

Hopeful that maybe the first floor fared as well, I stop at the head of the staircase and catch my breath. Sand everywhere. Furniture in the hall —smashed against the walls that have large holes in them, as if someone punched the wall with a fist. The front door is gone; I expected that. But it took most of the wall with it. Water flowed through so hard, so fast that it washed furniture—heavy pieces—as if they were toys. Few things are recognizable simply because the water picked them up and dashed them to pieces. I can't see the huge oak dining table, but I hope it's still in one piece.

One hand on the banister, I take each step cautiously. If the power of the waves could turn furniture into stick-sized pieces, then there's no telling what it might have done to the inside structure of the house. On the third step down, I step on sand. A thick layer. It's at that point I notice the wallpaper beside me. There's a distinct line running from the ground up to that level—about fifteen feet. My stomach threatens to turn out. Who can survive that high a water level if they don't have a tall place to get like the orphanage or the big brick buildings in the business district of Galveston down on the Strand? Like Mr. Cline and the weather service's office at the Levy building.

Careful not to slip, I make my way down the stairs, watching for anything threatening. But then, the whole house threatens me. It's not the comfortable safe place I lived in for over a year. Before I make it to the last step on to the first floor, a snake slithers across the hall from the parlor, heading to the tangle of lumber at the front door.

Snakes! I hate snakes! They don't belong in peoples' houses for sure. But they must have ridden the waves in from the dunes. A long cold shiver races down my backside. Everything we turn over or stick our hands into might have a snake hiding in it. This is the downside to the storm, I assume. Water, sand and snakes in the house. We'll be forever cleaning up this mess! Once on the first floor, I peak into the parlor. Even the mantle's been ripped off the wall though the walls seem sturdy enough. A smile lifts my mouth for the first time in days. Stuck up against a crack in the ceiling is that checker table Mr. Jack made. One leg must have gotten caught when the water filled the house. It floated up and got stuck. Thank goodness, something survived.

I try to remember what we were doing before the water and Winslow and the whole world washed away. Oh yeah, Ms. Christie sat in the chair on the other side of the checker table, doing embroidery. Something she said was mindless, that would keep her fingers busy and let her concentrate just enough not to worry about Mr. Jack. When he came in later, she laid that piecework, her needle, thimble, and tiny scissors down. Bet they're gone now, but at least one thing isn't a ruin.

My spirits lifted somewhat, I turn down the hall toward the back room, the back door and porch. But I don't move. Something...something I can't quite put my finger on...is wrong. We see sunshine coming in that door all the time. But not like this. As if nothing's blocking it. No kitchen or the two huge cottonwood trees that shade the tiny back yard. Suddenly those high spirits I captured a moment before, begin to slip out of me. My knees go a bit wobbly. For I see nothing as I come closer to the back of the house. Like the front door, the back door is gone along with part of the wall. The heavy table that saved my life is gone. The porch is gone. But then...

So is the kitchen building.

Gone are the trees. The barn beyond the kitchen. The workshop I should see at the far end of the next block. So is...everything! No houses for blocks. In the distance, only a smudge on the horizon. Galveston is gone!

FOREVER CHANGED

This time I don't throw up. I'm in too much shock. My imagination can never run a race with what I see before me. Nothing but piles of lumber solid for blocks. At least I think it's blocks. With nothing I recognize, I'm not even sure the back of the house still faces north. Once again, I smell salt, but then I'm standing in the sand that once lay on the beach at the edge of the tide. A mild breeze touches my cheek... apologizing for its bigger badder brother last night or just showing off? Grit covers my hands, and my boots stand in sand inches deep. Outside the hole that once was a door, I see the street. Or what was once a street. No water in sight. The waves have gone back to where they belong—in the gulf and the bay on the northeast side of the island.

What madness is this! Our homes. Our lives. Everything we cherish is changed forever! I recognize nothing!

"Jonathan?"

Damn, Ms. Christie's gonna want to come down and bring the children. I'm not sure how safe it is, with the snakes and the house. I've still got to go outside and see what's happening around us. I dread doing that. But if we are to stay and be as safe as possible I need to check.

Going back to the hall, I stop at the bottom of the steps and yell up to her, "Stay up there where it's dry and safe. The water level got almost to the second floor. The wind and water came through broken windows in the family rooms and pretty well soaked everything. Things aren't looking so good on the first floor. The flood made hash of everything. Furniture's busted. But that little ol' checker table is fine. You'll laugh when you see it. You need to watch out for snakes, ma'am. I've seen a few down here. Looks like they're trying to skedaddle, but there may still be some hiding among all this wreckage. Keep your eyes open. I'm going outside and see what the house looks like. Stay up there!" I insist. I can't imagine what she'll do when she sees not just the house—which can be cleaned and repaired, I hope—but the sight I can see outside the back door. Here's hoping the rest of the city doesn't look as bad.

"You hear me, ma'am?"

"We hear you, Jonathan. But—"

"No buts, ma'am. That's the way it has to be until I decide it's safe. Besides, Lawrence doesn't need to see all this." That ought to convince her.

"Right...you're right, Jonathan. We'll wait. Eat a little and drink a tiny bit of water."

"Wise idea, Ms. Christie. Those supplies may have to last a longer time than we planned on."

"You'll be back up soon?"

"Yes, ma'am." As soon as I determine if there's a reason why any of us should leave that attic.

———

After I walked what I thought was two blocks away from the water, I turn and look back at the boarding house. Sure enough, it floated off the blocks that kept it high and dry in normal rain and storms. What we just went through was anything but normal. The sun's high enough that I reckon it to be mid-morning. I don't see anyone else though. Boards and debris of all kinds cover the ground. I've yet to actually stand on grass or the dirt in the street.

The house leans a little back, pushed to the north by a unique wall of lumber, furniture...I can't even make out everything in that pile. The first boards must have hit the outside wall sideways and everything behind it stacked up higher and higher until the curved pile stands higher than the boarding house roof. To make the sight even stranger, the last few pieces of timber must have tried to go over like a shot of water, but stuck, so acted like a ramp that shot the water over the house instead of letting it fall directly on the attic and us. We'd have been dead but for that weird collection of...whatever is in that pile leaning against the front of the house. Taking all that down will be dangerous. The timbers could slip, and the house be crushed.

A few steps to my left gives me another view of the house. My mind is numb with realization that I should be seeing the kitchen, the barn with its cranky old horses and the workshop taking up most of the corner of the block. Nothing...nothing is there that I knew from before. A few steps to my right and I step on something soft. The first thing soft. I lift my shoe to see what's beneath it and jump back! A hand! Someone's buried under the boards I've been standing on!

Frantically I start pushing and pulling boards aside, but within less than a minute, I realize the person beneath needs no saving. What's left of a man is long dead, his face rubbed raw from sand, wind and waves.

"Son! You all right?" Someone has rounded the corner of the boarding house, sees me and shouts.

"Doing all right, sir, but..." I point to the dead person at my feet. "I think this fella is past help."

The man makes his way to me, watching where he steps. Boards shift when you walk, as I discovered. He takes a quick look at the corpse but shakes his head. "I came from over on Avenue M...at least I think that's where I started. Ain't nothing left to tell a body where they are. A few places like here still standing but all crooked-like." He rubs his head, apparently not realizing he's bleeding.

"Don't do that, sir," I catch his hand before he can rub a wide gap that's no longer bleeding but lies open. "You've cut yourself. If you keep doing that you might make it worse."

"No joke?" He acts like he can't feel it. Maybe he can't. Frankly I'm having a hard time putting my mind to all this.

The longer we stand there, the more folks gather round. Not more than a dozen and they all come from different directions, trying to find their folks or home. Most are rough dressed, wet, bedraggled. A few got picked up by waves and are lucky to be alive, though their clothes are nearly gone. We share shirts, so folks at least look decent.

"How far's the damage?" I ask the group of men standing around with me. No women have appeared so far.

"Damage? Far? Son, there's no Galveston left!" one man says in a thick voice. "You can count the number of places still standing on two hands and maybe one foot. Might be some of those fancy businesses on the Strand or Broadway are still standing. I don't know. All I know is we got us a problem. Few places to put folks when night comes that's safe. Food. Water. Clothes," he adds as he fingers what's left of his pants and shirt—tattered rags hanging from a body that's bruised up.

"Ain't the only problem we got," adds a man standing not far away. "Take a deep breath."

We all start but wind up coughing. "Those that died are going to rot pretty quick in this infernal September heat. We gotta get them picked up and buried."

"How many folks you think we lost?" one innocent asks.

"Look around you, man. Houses and businesses gone. Where are the folks that lived in them? Worked in them? Gone to a church or brick place or school to be safe? I hope so 'cause if not, there's gonna be a lot of bodies to bury before nightfall."

"And the next problem is," I pause to collect my thoughts before speaking since I'm the youngest one in the group. "Finding all those folks in this pile of timbers and shingles and downed trees and fencing. We'll be digging for days."

"By then the smell's gonna be over-powering."

"We need to find those still alive though. Anyone got any idea how to feed them folks or find water for them?" one man asks.

This time I keep my mouth shut. If these fellas find out Ms. Christie's got supplies laid up for just this sort of emergency, then they may rush her to get them.

No one has an answer to that question. I make a move back toward the boarding house. My dread now is telling Ms. Christie what the city has become—a place of devastation and possible disease. A place where maybe more are missing than are alive.

How can I tell her that? Assure her that those we care for are all right? I think the best way to let her know is to take her to the back door and let her see for herself the way Galveston looks now. Her home is a lucky one; it still stands. Few others do.

What if she asks me about finding Mr. Jack and Jackie? How can anyone find anything in this tumbled landscape?

Best I get back before she decides to come looking for me. With a heavy heart and a mind numbed by what I've seen, I make my way toward the back of the house, pausing for a few minutes to make sure the barn and horses really aren't there anymore. Checking that everything above the foundation piers of the kitchen has disappeared. One last long glance back to the far corner a block away where I should see the tall building that houses the Zimmerman Furniture workshop—it, too, no longer exists. I fear that much of the city as I knew it two day ago will never return.

————

One of the hardest things I ever do is take Ms. Christie—and the children —to the first floor and into the big back room, to the open space that once was a door. I hold Mattie in one arm and hold Louise's hand. Ms. Christie refuses to give up Lawrence, though he's a heavy load, lying lax in her arms. Like he's off somewhere in his own world. Breathing but not paying attention to what's going on around him.

"But..." She stutters, her eyes wide, her mouth open, her hands opening, closing on Lawrence's jacket. "But there's nothing out there."

"Yes, ma'am. If you went outside and looked around, you'd find out there's not a lot left of the city. Maybe we just got hit the hardest, but I doubt it. I met up with some fellas who walked over from near Broadway. Some of those mansions survived and a few churches. But as they got closer to the beach, there's not a lot left."

"But the people?" She's having as much trouble accepting this as I am.

"Don't know, ma'am. But there are dead out there." I'm not about to tell her how I know from personal experience. "Lots of folks to bury, I reckon, and it's gonna have to be done quick."

As if to reinforce what I just said, the wind shifts a bit, and we all wrinkle our noses. Mid-afternoon Sunday now, no one's going to church, even if there was one left. But the Lord's work of finding and giving the dead a proper burial remains.

"Best you and the younguns get back upstairs. Snakes probably still wiggling around down here. Hope there's not any on the second floor, but we'll have to worry about that as we go along." I try to hustle her back down the hall, but she stops and asks the one thing I hoped she'd not.

"What about my husband? And my son?"

I do what I've seen Mr. Jack do a hundred times. I step up to her, hug her with one arm and give her a quick kiss on the forehead. "I'm not sure, ma'am, but I'll do what I can to find them."

For a second, she lays her head on my shoulder, but we can't stay down here. I have to figure out how to board up the doors—at least the back door. I need an ax and some heavy gloves. And a kerchief...to cover my nose while I work. Because what's bad now is gonna get worse—fast.

———

By Monday morning, men come past, pushing debris out of the way, to make room for carts—death carts. So many bodies floated in the bay and lay stranded among the timbers that burial wasn't possible. A man named Fayling came by, telling us he was in charge of all the militia. He'd have no looting, sightseers, thrill seekers or reporters. Like any of us trying to dig our way out of this disaster worry about that. We want our lives back. I'd say *back to normal,* but I don't think *normal* will ever be like it was this time last week. The sun's barely up, but I've got to clear the front of the house in order to insure it's safe.

So far, we've not heard from McGraw or Thrill. We think they made it to Houston, so might be safe. Ms. Christie does worry about Mr. Fuller though, same as me. He's a nice man who owns a hardware store nearer the Strand. Could be he's still there, or maybe he...we don't talk about the alternative.

Ms. Christie still sits in the attic, holding Lawrence. She won't come down, while he's so weak. He doesn't speak. His eyelids are barely open. If prayer could heal that little man, he'd be dancing in the street. As if any prayer's gonna help. I resigned myself to that fact same as I did last night when a man came by just before sundown on his way uptown to the German Catholic church on Broadway. The place suffered little damage as the particular street, running east and west along the middle of the island, is the highest place in the city.

He stopped to find out how my folks fared. A kerchief covered his nose as well. "Most unbelievable thing I ever saw," he started the conversation.

"What's that, Mr. Angus?" He'd introduced himself as Myron Angus.

"St. Mary's Orphanage out on the beach...gone!"

At that word, I dropped the ax I'd found and grabbed him. "What do you mean *gone*? My brother lived there!"

"Ah gee, fella, I'm sorry. The whole place is wiped off the map like it was never there. No buildings. No animals. No people. But I did hear..." He stopped and gave me a sideways glance. When he took a step away from me, I realized he wasn't going to finish whatever he started. I reached out and grabbed his arm.

With all the courage I could muster, I demanded he tell me what he heard.

"Fella told me the bay is full of bodies. They seen the nuns, with those little ones tied to their waists with rope. All dead." He shook off my arm and murmured as he left. "Sorry, young fella."

I remember I plopped down on a stump that'd floated by and landed near the house. Georgie? Gone? Dead? My words came back to haunt me. 'That ol' gulf's gonna swaller you up some day'. How I wish I'd never said that.

Once more, I dragged myself back to the attic, delivering more bad news to Ms. Christie. Not the news any of us wanted to hear. But she held me and let me cry until I lay down with the other children and dreamed—my dreams filled, perhaps like theirs, with memories of better days.

———

"Ma'am?" I've called her three times from the bottom of the staircase on the first floor. I hear Mattie crying. "Louise?"

"Jonathan, Mama's crying funny-like. You gotta come." Her once-rowdy voice is now toned down to a fair quiet one.

Ms. Christie crying now can only mean one thing. Lawrence—either he's gone or dying in her arms. Mondays aren't usually a good day anyway. This Monday will go down in history as the worst as far as I'm concerned. Now this. I dread what I might find as I gallop up the stairs, two at a time.

Sure enough, Ms. Christie sits in a patch of sunshine holding the quilt that kept Lawrence warm. Only now, she's rocking back and forth, sobbing quiet-like. One arm holds him to her while the other pats him as if rocking him gently to sleep. This time I fear she's rocking him for the last time.

"Ma'am?" I kneel down in front of her, then reach out and pull the corner of the quilt away from Lawrence's face. Sure enough, the little fella's done give out. Gone. Dead. "Ms. Christie? What do we do now?" Honestly, I have no idea what to do with the body. I can't think of him as Lawrence anymore even when tears wash down my face and speaking is so hard.

Louise holds Mattie near the doorway. She's been crying, too; I can see her face all puffy and red. But now she's numb. I guess that's how it is when half of you dies. That's what Mr. Jack told me about twins once. They're two halves of a whole.

"Ma'am. We gotta take him..." Where? We can't bury Lawrence. That's not possible. I turn cold and shiver as a result when I think of the only possible alternative to burying...the death carts. Ms. Christie's not seen them or heard of them yet.

Work crews are rounding up the dead and loading them into carts to be taken to a barge. From there, the bodies will be weighted and buried at sea. Good enough for sailors, I suppose, but not for a little boy barely five years old. Still I can think of no other plan.

Ms. Christie will refuse. I know that as certain as I know tomorrow is Tuesday.

"Ma'am, men are gathering up the dead, taking them to a barge to be buried at sea. We can't bury them on the island. There's too many. Burial at sea is a clean way to go. If those bodies stay here, disease will break out, and we'll all get sick. We survived that storm. We can't get ill and die now. You've got two little girls that need you. We might find Mr. Jack and Jackie. We have to be strong for them, too." I say anything I can think of in order to make her see we can't hold onto the body. Lawrence is just a body now. What made that little man *Lawrence* is gone.

Outside, I hear the sound of rolling wheels, men talking, a wail from far off as if a woman cries out. The death carts are coming. I have to get Lawrence away from his mother and down to the street.

"Let me take him, Ms. Christie. He's not here anymore. He's in that Heaven you always talk about." I ease my arms toward her, slipping them in under the body that's now growing stiff. Ever so slowly, I curl my arms up against her, as if we both hold him. Which we are. The trick now is making her let go. "Let me have him, ma'am. I'll take care of him." I try to pull him away from Ms. Christie, but she's having none of it. "The carts are coming, ma'am. He's gotta go with 'em."

"I'll carry him down," she says low. "Help me up. Louise, stay here with Mattie. I'll return shortly."

Between the two of us, she manages to stand, still holding the quilt-wrapped body. Like a soldier determined to do her duty, she carries her last son down the stairs to the back door. There she lets me take Lawrence while she sits on the floor, then jumps the three feet down to the ground. But she holds out her arms to me, her face so stricken, with tears silently now rolling down her cheeks to drip off her jaw, that I have no choice but to surrender the dear bundle.

I help her maneuver her way to the back yard where the gate might have been. But here I stop her. She can't, under any circumstances, see those carts.

In the distance, I see three of them. The smell in the yard alone is making me sick. People and animals are beginning to decay in the day's heat. The memory of that raging storm diminishes slightly in the face of what we now face.

"Ma'am, I know you want to lay out Lawrence yourself, but, ma'am, the carts aren't for you to see." Her heart would break to see the bodies, most naked from tumbling in the waves for hours. Many bodies suffered severe damage as well. Those carts aren't a pretty sight, and only brave men deal with them. I'm not brave enough, for sure.

"Turn your back, Ms. Christie. Turn around," I say as I take her by the shoulders and turn her back to the street. Bad enough that she'll catch the smell, but the sight is so much worse.

"Jonathan." Someone speaks right behind me, low in a wondering-sort of voice. I turn fast and all but stumble into Samuel.

"Samuel! You're alive!" I hug him something fierce. While he returns my embrace, I can tell something's wrong. I hold his shoulders but step back, so I can see his face. Horror, torture, everything imaginable that's bad is stamped across his features. A gentle boy, this storm has ripped out part of his soul, if I'm any judge. And now... "Samuel, tell me you're not working with the carts?" To survive...only to do this? I can't imagine what that's like for my best friend.

He nods but doesn't speak further. As if too many horrible sights have piled up in his mind, he's numb. And now I have to add one more thing to his load.

Thankfully, Ms. Christie is so wrapped up in her own sorrow that she's not heard me and Samuel. But perhaps she'll do better if she hands over the small body to someone who knew Lawrence. I have to ask her, but I feel like I'm betraying Samuel...to ask him to do this one thing that will help ease her heart but load his.

"Samuel, would you help us?"

He nods, but his eyes are far away.

"Lawrence died this morning. His little heart gave way. Ms. Christie knows she has to let go of him, so he can be buried at sea, but I'm afeared she might not give him up. She might if she knows you'll take the boy. It's a hard thing I ask you to do." I'm not adding to his burden by telling him about Mr. Jack, Jackie, or Georgie. "Will you help us?"

He nods again and moves past me, headed to Ms. Christie. The carts are almost to us. The smell almost takes my breath. Around Samuel's neck, I see a handkerchief. A powerful smell passes me as he does. Camphor! These men wear kerchiefs that have been soaked or somehow have camphor in them to cut the smell. Samuel must have pulled his kerchief down when he came ahead of the carts to find me.

He stands in front of her, his arms out. I move up behind her but stay quiet. This is between them.

"I'll take him, Ms. Christie. He'll be safe with me."

The carts rumble by, rolling to a slow death march. Soon they'll be past us. Will she surrender the boy or not?

"Please, ma'am. I have to take him. I promise. He'll be safe with me." Samuel stands like a black statue, his face older by years than the last time I saw him. I forgot to ask if his family is safe, but that's something I can ask when he returns. He reaches for the body.

"Jonathan?" I pull myself away from those two to find...

"Mr. Granger...good to see you alive, sir." Mr. Granger is one of Mr. Jack's customers. Not rich or anything, but someone who has bought a few small things for his wife who is so ill she lays in bed all day. "Your family, sir?"

He hangs his head. "I lost Martha and Lulu when the storm broke up the house. I managed to hold on to an oak, but I've not found any of my family since we began this..." He points to the carts.

"You're helping with the bodies?" I put my hand on his shoulder and give it a gentle squeeze. "I'm sorry about your family, sir."

"You got someone we need to pick up?"

"Samuel...my best friend...is about to get a little boy. He died after the storm, but I don't know if his mama is strong enough to let the child go."

"I understand. Tell Samuel to follow as soon as possible." Head still down, he passes on down the street, following the last cart. Now and then, one stops, and someone brings out a body. Too sick to watch, I turn back to the drama in my own back yard.

As I do, I see Ms. Christie slide the quilted form over into Samuel's arms. She trusts him enough to care for the boy properly. As he leaves, she hangs her head, places her hands over her face and sobs so loudly I fear her heart's abreakin'.

Perhaps that's the last straw for my friend. I can see his anguish. But he never lets Ms. Christie see how much his soul suffers.

Samuel never looks at me as he passes, the body held up against his chest as if Lawrence is sleeping. His gaze never meets mine, as if he's got this one thing on his mind. I watch him though as I move up behind Ms. Christie. To my surprise, she turns and buries her head against my neck. I let her cry as Samuel walks behind the last cart, that precious bundle held close. As far as I can see them, and that's for blocks, he never lays the body up on the cart. Instead, he marches like a lost soul behind, still holding the body. No one tells him to put it in the cart apparently. It's a small thing but makes my heart lighter to know someone who loved Lawrence is carrying him to his final resting place.

———

Tuesday evening, only days after the storm. News comes slowly as men pass by. I see women walking, as if out for a Sunday stroll, but their lost expressions tell the truth. They no longer recognize their city. They can't even recognize the block where they lived. Still, as hopeless as the affair seems, men work side by side, pulling away debris. First, they looked for survivors. Now they look for bodies while removing rubble in order to rebuild.

"Jonathan," comes a hiss. I'm beyond tired. I've spent the past two days removing debris from around the house. Others have stopped by to help. I can't repay them in any way other than to offer my thanks and say I'll help them in return as soon as I know the house is safe for the family.

"Mr. Granger? You made it back from that..." How can I describe the burial detail he was assigned to perform? We both leave words like that unsaid.

"Look, young fella, I visited with that friend of yours...that black boy, Samuel. He carried that little boy's body the entire way to the barge. No one bothered him 'cause...well, I don't think he was with us anymore. You know what I'm trying to say?" Granger looks years older than when I saw him the day before.

"Yeah, I do, sir. I could tell Samuel saw too much horrible stuff during the storm. I never got to ask him if his family was all right or not. He just looked like he didn't care anymore."

"You got that about right. His family made it to a church, and they're all right, but I had to go tell them..." He turns his flat cap round and round in his hands, never giving me a direct glance.

Something begins gnawing in my guts. Please don't tell me something happened to Samuel. I'm not sure I'm brave enough to lose someone else I care for. But that storm either killed, damaged or left mangled souls behind to rebuild. In this case, it damaged a tender soul. One that might not have survived the atrocities.

"Just tell me straight up, sir," I sigh, not really wanting to hear the news but suspecting the worse.

"Samuel helped load the barge but laid that quilted body aside. When we were loaded—took us longer than we thought it would—he picked up that little boy and carried him aboard. Then he sat next to coiled ropes and the weights we'd loaded—staring off into space, cuddling that body to him. The plan was to weigh down each body and dump 'em overboard. The weight would take them to the bottom. Didn't work out that way, but that came after Samuel's story. I took up a seat close by, worried-like for the boy. Him being black didn't matter. This was a person hurting. I watched over him after we talked—wasn't much but enough. But I fell asleep. We went out near twenty miles, but by the time we got out it was dark...too late to do...what we had to do."

His face green, Granger swallows a few times before continuing. "We had to spend the night out there with that barge-load of bodies. That alone's enough to drive a person to drink. But for that boy—it must have been too much. I woke up when I heard a splash. Being the gulf and all, I didn't think anything about it. I didn't realize what happened. Drifted back to sleep but when the sun started to break, and men started stirring, one of 'em asked where was the black boy and that body he clutched all day. We searched the barge but didn't find what we was looking for. I checked the area where he sat all night and discovered rope and maybe a hundred-fifty pounds of weights gone. Can't imagine how he managed to do it all but he and that little boy took a plunge over the rail and with all that weight—well, they never came up." He pauses, then adds a more horrifying detail. "Unlike the bodies we dumped that all came back to shore with the tide today." Granger suddenly sits, practically falls into a heap on the street, his legs given out. From telling that tale, I suspect.

"All the bodies, sir?" My imagination runs wild with that picture.

"We think all—but for that boy Samuel and the little one he took with him. I had to tell his maw and paw what we think happened. Though they were shocked at the news, I don't think it surprised them. They were just shocked that he chose that way to go. Understand what I mean?"

"Yeah, I think I do." I raise my eyes to the attic window—what's left of it. Ms. Christie stands there with Mattie in her arms. Louise stands next to her. They wave to me. I give them a smile and return the wave, though my heart's not in it.

Granger lowers his head and sighs, a breath so heavy it makes my heart hurt. "Even the gulf denies those poor people a decent burial."

"What's gonna happen to the bodies now?"

"Burning."

"What did you say?" Surely, I didn't hear him say they'd burn the bodies.

"The bodies from now on will be gathered and burned. Nothing else we can do. Can't bury them here on the island. Too damn many. Can't bury them at sea...the gulf spits 'em back at us. So funeral pyres are the last resort." In the setting sun, Granger looks old, sick, and green.

"I think this is something I'll take to my grave, sir. About Samuel, I mean. Ms. Christie trusted Samuel to take care of her boy, but she's not needing to hear how he did it. Or that he took his own life in keeping that promise. Or that bodies will be burned now. She'll find out soon enough when that smell spreads over the island." I glance back at the window. Only Louise stands there now, her arms crossed over a broken piece of board I wedged up there, so she and Mattie wouldn't fall out the gaping hole. In her hand, I see a crust of bread. Thankful now that Ms. Christie had the idea of putting together those provisions, Louise, Mattie and she can eat and drink and not starve like some of those I've seen in the past two days.

Mr. Granger pats my knee where I squat next to him. "Wise decision, son. Few knew the boy. Not even his name. I took it upon myself to tell his parents. Nobody else seemed to care enough. They're about as soul-sore as me. I'm sure not to tell the missus myself. Well," he says as he pulls himself up, "best I get back to the shelter and get some rest. A new crew's working now. We can't do just day shifts. Too many dead. Thirty-minute shifts all day...all night. Heat's not helping any."

"I understand, sir. I wish you the best." We shake hands, and he heads up Avenue L...or what's left of it. He never said where he's sheltering, and I never thought to ask. I got problems of my own.

———

"Ma'am, I think you need to take the girls and go to Houston as soon as you can. You'll be safe there," I argue yet again Tuesday night.

"No, Jonathan. The girls and I are staying. We still haven't found Jack or Jackie. They could still be alive, stuck in a tree like those boys from the orphanage." Seeing my stricken face, she hugs me. "Oh, my dear, I'm so sorry. I forgot! Georgie wasn't with them, but..." She gives my arm an encouraging squeeze. "He could have survived, and we just haven't found him yet. Like my husband and son," she repeats. "We just have to hold out 'til help arrives."

That's what she's said for two days now. *I'm staying*, she says over and over. *You need to leave*, I tell her over and over. We're not making progress in the direction I want her to go. I think we're here on the island for the long haul.

Wednesday morning, I decide to take a walk around and see for myself what's going on. Among the smells of decay, smells of funeral fires will start soon.

"Keep the girls inside, ma'am. You, too. You might start working on the bedrooms. But watch out for snakes. I've come across a dozen or more by now while clearing the front of the house." We can finally see out the front windows and doors...or where they once were. I plan to use some of the timbers I've pried off to wedge into place and create a safer place for them.

"I want to walk to Broadway, then to the Strand if I can make it that far. I'll be careful. I got good boots and this here ax. You've got your board and nail." I'd found a right-sized board with a long nail sticking through the end while cleaning. Slow work to say the least. I brought the board in and gave it to her as protection. She can swing it and stick that rusted nail in someone to take him out or at least slow down a body. Still I worry about leaving them alone.

"I'd take y'all with me, but I'm afeared what you might see. The girls are too little to walk that far, so best you stay here. Don't stay in the attic. If someone comes after you, you don't want to be trapped in the highest spot in the house. Stay on the second floor. The first is still covered in sand and probably still has a few snakes and other varmints."

During all this, Ms. Christie stands quietly, her hands clasped in front of her. By now, her denim jeans are dirty, and her blouse is dingy with dirt. Her jacket covers her girls at night. Mud streaks the girls' faces, but neither of them seems to mind. I recall when Georgie would play all day and come in of an evening and squawk like a chicken when Maw would clean him up. He saw nothing wrong with a little dirt.

I gather up my jacket and ax, wishing I still had my flat cap. Nothing for it but to take foot in hand and get moving. The sooner I leave, the sooner I'll be back.

"You gonna take something to eat?"

"Can't afford to walk around with a poke full of food, ma'am. Might get robbed. Some of that going around."

"Right you are, sir. At least take this crust of bread and eat it before you go. Drink this, too." She offers me a thick slice of bread and a cup from one of the jugs of water. Both of us know this won't last much longer. The two of us eat light, so the girls can have enough.

"Thank you, ma'am," I say as she walks down the stairs with me. By now, the girls know to stay in the attic. "I'll be home before dark for sure."

"Jonathan, keep your eyes open for Mr. Jack and Jackie."

"You bet, ma'am." I try to sound right cheerful, but we're losing hope that either of them survived. At least I am. I'm not sure Ms. Christie will ever stop hoping for their survival.

"Oh, and will you pass by Mr. Fuller's hardware store?"

"I can."

"Do and see how it fared. See if he's all right. Let him know how we're doing...that I plan to level and repair this place and get it going again. He's welcomed back when we open." Her positive cheerfulness grates on me. What hope do we have that anyone we know survived that storm?

Still I can't deny her. "I can do that, ma'am," I repeat.

She stops me at the bottom of the steps and takes my jacket. Like a good hostess, she holds it, so I can slip my arms in. Then she turns me around and smooths my hair. "There. You look...wait!" Like a kid, she scampers back up the stairs.

Puzzled I wait, but grin when she returns minutes later carrying a flat cap in dark brown.

"This is one of Jack's caps." She sets it on my head, and I instinctively tug it into place. "Now that's the Jonathan I know." Her arms come around me and hugs me tight. "Be careful, please. We do so need you."

I return her hug, then tug my cap in salute. "Yes, ma'am." With a wave, I'm off to explore what's left of Galveston, Texas.

———

"Mr. Fuller...Tilman!" Ms. Christie hugs the hardware man so hard I'm afeared he's gonna choke. "You're all right? Your store? Your employees?" She waves him to the stairs leading to the attic, about the only place left to sit that isn't covered with sand and things no one recognizes.

The girls come to sit with us. They sit on each side of their maw, while I sit one step down, tickling Mattie's legs. Her giggles are a welcome relief after all I've seen today.

We settle to find out what's happened to Mr. Fuller.

"I left here Saturday and went to my shop. I closed it Friday night and told my helpers to stay home until the storm passed, then we'd open back up, thinking people would need our supplies to make any repairs. Water came in the doors soon after I arrived. I made an attempt to move smaller things that might suffer from salt water to the second floor. But I couldn't work as fast as the water was rising. Being wedged between two brick buildings saved my place. But there's so much damage to what was in the store. My goods were either washed away or ruined. Basically, I have to start over again, but at least I have a building that's still standing and in fair shape." He claps me on the shoulder. "I was never so glad as to see Jonathan this morning. There's little in my place to steal, and the militia is stringent about stopping looters, saying looters will be shot on sight, so I thought it would be safe to join him, checking out the rest of the city. At least as much as we can make in one day on foot." His face is as grimy as ours. His clothes as dirty. But he appears hungry.

"Have you eaten or had anything to drink, sir?" Ms. Christie still has the ability to read my mind and picks up on his needs right fast.

"No, ma'am. I had a sip or two of water, but nothing to eat in several days. I never dreamed I'd wind up in this kind of situation," he admits with a sort of disbelieving headshake.

"Us either," I agree as Ms. Christie hops up, leaving the girls with us.

"Be right back," she says and gallops up the attic stairs. In less than two minutes, she returns with two slices of bread coated with thick molasses as well as two cups of water. "Here." She hands one slice and cup to Fuller and gives me the other slice and cup. "I know Jonathan is hungry. He's always ready to eat. And he's had a bit to eat and drink every day." She tucks her arms over her legs and leans forward, watching as we both feast on something as simple as bread and water.

Fuller finishes his meal and leans back against the wall. "I can't compare that to Ms. Vassy's meals, ma'am, but that was better than anything she ever cooked."

Another one of those silences falls over us. It happens now and then when Ms. Christie or I mention someone like Vassy or Juliet or one of the men who work in the furniture workshop. We have no idea if they survived, though hope is playing out that they did. Otherwise, they would have contacted us. Besides, most of those folks lived down on the east end of the island, close to the beach. Nothing's left down at that end of the island.

"Do you have a place to stay in the evenings, Mr. Fuller?" asks Ms. Christie.

"Please, ma'am, after all this, call me Tilman."

"Quite right, sir...Tilman. We're Christie, Jonathan, Louise and Mattie. Friends all around," she says as she pats each of us on the shoulder. "But as I asked, do you have a place to stay?"

"My building is sound enough, and I have a cot upstairs. I sleep there."

"Ah, that's good. I wish I could offer the house, but as you can see, we're a bit tilted at the moment," she says with a chuckle. "As soon as I get leveled out," she breaks to laugh at her little joke, "you must return."

"Your place needs more attention than mine. Maybe I can come by and help clean up when things calm down. Right now, folks are still in shock, and without clean water or facilities or food of any kind, I'm afraid many aren't thinking straight."

My mind immediately flashes to the last time I saw Samuel. Food and water had nothing to do with his thinking, but it sure wasn't straight.

"Travel takes a bit on foot, avoiding debris and workers and such, but I'll return every day or so and check on you, if I may?"

"That would be lovely," Ms. Christie says. "Perhaps when you return one of these days, Jack will be back."

"He's not here?" Mr. Fuller must have thought Mr. Jack off working somewhere.

"No, he..." She stops and slaps a hand over her mouth while sucking in air.

I know she'll cry if she has to explain what happened.

"Mr. Jack met up with Mr. Winslow downstairs just as the storm busted over the island. Things didn't go so well. Mr. Winslow left the house maybe a minute before one of those big swells came in the front door and out the back. The current swept Mr. Jack and his oldest son, Jackie, right out the door. We haven't seen them since."

"I am so sorry." Mr. Fuller—Tilman—offers his sympathies quietly.

I see his eyes glance around, counting children. If Mr. Jack is gone... And Jackie's gone... And there's only us, then where's...?

"And young Lawrence?" He knows something happened and hates to ask. I can see that in his eyes.

"Died. He had a bad heart. The storm was too much for him to bear."

This time, Tilman Fuller can find no words, though he drops his head. In the silence, we hear him praying for Lawrence's soul and the fast return of Mr. Jack and Jackie.

"Tilman, it's late. Perhaps you best return before the curfew," Ms. Christie suggests.

She's not one for reliving sad memories so wants him gone for the day. Perhaps another day she'll be strong enough to talk about her family without her heart pouring out through tears on her cheeks.

"Yes, yes, you're right. Best I get home. Well, back to my store. But I'll return if I may?"

"Please do. A familiar face will be welcomed."

"Jonathan, you can walk me out and show me what you've done to keep house and hearth over the family," Tilman suggests.

"Yes, sir." I stand and lead the way out the back door. "I'll be back in a few minutes," I call back to Ms. Christie.

"Take care among all that rubble," she returns.

We move carefully to the front of the boarding house. The majority of the boards still lean against the house, but I've cleared enough to let sunshine in through windows and door. "The main thing right now is keeping this mess from pushing the house over. If I can get help, we can move most of this off in a day or two. Then it just remains to somehow level the place."

"The house looks odd, doesn't it? Sitting all tilted off its foundation like that." Tilman bends over and studies the pilings that used to support the house a good five feet off the ground. "This whole island's going to have to do something. We can't live in fear that another storm like that might wipe us off the map like this one tried to do. I don't want to rebuild and maybe marry and have a family someday only to see it all lost because we're sitting bare feet above the tide line."

I agree, but being only fifteen, few would listen to me. Besides, he knows what needs doing.

Tilman turns to me, and a smile eases the tension on his face. "Jonathan, I'm glad you made it to my place. I had no idea the damage was so bad. I'm glad I walked with you. Best you get back inside now and tell Ms. Christie what all you saw."

We shake hands, glad to have met up, hoping for a brighter future than we can see at the moment.

———

"You Jonathan Evans?" A boy about my age calls to me. I'm on the far side of the house today trying to clear away more debris. Progress is slow, but I can see that things are looking better. At times, I leave my house and help neighbors. About three houses along both sides of our street survived the storm's rage though like the Zimmerman house, each one sits at a cockeyed angle.

"That's me. What can I do for you?" I come down from a pile of timber and offer my hand.

We shake, and he says, "Mr. Cranston—Thomas he says to tell you—sent me to find you. Says it's about his boss, Mr. Jack. The man said to tell only you. Not to tell the lady. He says you're to come quick."

Mr. Jack! Is he alive? Hurt? Surely not dead. Ms. Christie can't take it if the man she loves is dead. Bad enough that one son is missing and the other is dead. To lose the foundation of her life will about kill her.

"Is Mr. Jack alive? Did Thomas say?" I'm scrambling down the pile now.

"He didn't say. Just said to get you fast as a shot. I'm to bring you to where he is."

"I'll be with you as soon as I can," I tell him. "Don't go anywhere. Don't let the lady see you either," I warn.

"Right. I'll wait right here."

How to get away from Ms. Christie without telling her why I'm rushing off so fast? I can't just go without telling her I'm not out front working. Life is tense enough right now without making matters worse.

"Ms. Christie?" I rush in but try to straighten up my face, so she doesn't do that mind reading thing she's so good at.

Sally Turner is upstairs with Ms. Christie, and they both come down to the second-floor landing and look over the grimy railing. Mrs. Turner and her husband lived down the street. They went to the Catholic church Friday night. She's a timid lady and didn't feel safe in her home. Smart lady, seeing as her house on the corner is no longer there. She came by with her husband earlier in the day. Mr. Turner is helping others on the street in cleaning up. Mrs. Turner stopped in to visit with Ms. Christie. I'm glad because Ms. Christie's missed the company of women folk something fierce.

"Yes, Jonathan?"

"I gotta go out for a bit. I'll be right back." I try to act like leaving for a few minutes isn't so important.

Ms. Christie wrinkles her forehead. A sure sign she's thinking. "What's the matter?"

"Nothing, ma'am. Only someone needs my help. Best I go see what's happening, so I can decide if I need to help right now or it can wait, that's all," I say as I grab my jacket and cap. "Be back soon," I call and head out the back door.

Fast as I can, I circle the house on the far side, not the street side. If she's the least bit suspicious, she'll be watching for me there.

"Come on. Take me to Thomas," I tell the boy as I grab him by the shirtsleeve. "Let's move before Ms. Christie shows up. I'm not sure she's convinced I'm on the up and up."

How this guy knows where he's going I have no idea. We veer off to the west, an area I've not explored yet. The destruction here is bad enough, but in the spots where the storm did the most damage there's simply nothing left. The Episcopal church is almost totally ruined. I can't even see folks working to clear rubble. What are we doing out here?

Debris is stacked high in many areas. Mounds twenty feet high used to be houses, stores, barns. The smell is stout. I close my mind to what might lie among the rubble.

We round a tall stack, at least a good six feet higher than my head, and I spot Thomas standing with three other men. A sight for sore eyes, he, too, looks like times haven't done well by him.

"Thomas!"

He sees me and opens his arms. Like a kindly grandfather, he embraces me, holds me longer than I thought he might. That alone tells me he's lost someone. Maybe all. I hold him as long as he wants. If a shudder of a sob passes between us, that's all right.

At last, he releases me and takes a fast swipe at his eyes. "Good to see you, lad. Granger told me you and the missus survived. The children?"

"Only the girls. Jackie...well, that's a story for later. Young Lawrence had a bad heart. I never knew. The storm did him in. He died Monday morning."

"Aw, I'm that sorry to hear about the little boy. The girls are all right?"

"Yes, sir. We don't know about Mr. Jack or Jackie yet though. The first wave that broke through the house swept them away. Mr. Jack was... hurt before it hit, and he couldn't save himself or the child."

"Ah, as to Mr. Jack. Uh, Jonathan. I think I can help. But, son, it's a gruesome sight. Can you bear up? Will you be strong?"

He's telling me Mr. Jack is dead. And Thomas found the body.

"I can't tell you I'll be strong, Thomas. I loved the man like a father. Better than my own paw," I admit as the meager breakfast I had that morning swirls in my stomach, threatening to rise to my throat. The stench fills my nose. Sea birds swoop and call out, screeching like rusty nails across metal. The day's heat seeps into my bones but not enough to warm the chill that settles around my heart.

"Lead me to him, Thomas," I finally say.

Thomas takes me by the arm and leads me around the mound of debris. The others follow though the boy's taken off. "Look," Thomas says soft-like.

I look but see nothing. Nothing I expect to see. Nothing I recognize. "Where?"

"Look there, among the boards, deep in," he urges and holds on to me as I take a few steps forward. Suddenly my eyes make sense of what I'm seeing. I scream! Back up. Cover my mouth, swallowing to keep my stomach down. "Is that...?"

"Yes, son. I found him among the boards when we were clearing away the debris. Disease is gonna set in if we don't get the bodies out. Whether it be man or beast. And there's plenty of them as well."

I inch forward again, my eyes almost unable to put face to features sagging and lax. Naked, Jack Zimmerman lies tangled among the timbers, his arms stretched out like those of Christ on the cross. Boards hide his private parts but from the way sand and surf battered him, there's probably not anything of that kind left. His face is distorted almost as if he still lived when trapped. Without studying him too close, I see that he's lost one eye. His lips are torn, and part of his nose is gone. I recognize him though, same as Thomas, despite the state he's in now. His arms lay sprawled among the boards, while his legs are together, straight. One thing is painfully obvious even in the decayed body.

All eyes are on me. I feel them boring a hole in my back.

"Jonathan, can you explain the bullet hole in Mr. Jack's chest?" Thomas asks.

"Yes," I say with all the bitterness buried in me. "I can. And the man who did that will pay if he's not dead already."

"Oh, he's not dead, dear boy. Not by a long shot," comes a voice from behind us.

Before I can turn to face Lazarus Winslow, that murderer, he grabs me around the neck from behind and sticks a gun to my head.

"How the hell did you survive when a good man like Jack Zimmerman died? You bastard!" I yell, even as Winslow tightens his hold and pushes the gun harder to my temple.

"Quiet, Jonny," he almost sings. "I always survive. That raid. You, the snake, who wormed your way into Jack Zimmerman's good graces when it should have been me who warmed his heart." A nasty laugh fills my ear. "I even survived that hellacious storm. But," he digs the gun into my head, "my lover didn't. Jack had him killed in the raid."

"Your people started shooting!" I try to get out but break off with a cry of pain. "Awww!"

"And now that this hideous man is dead, dear boy, the only one left to finish off is you," he leans over, his gun to my head, all the while apparently keeping a close watch on Thomas and the other men.

They stand like statues, knowing—same as me—that the man behind me will shoot. Thomas knows Winslow. The others don't. "Let him go, Winslow. He's done nothing to you."

"Ah, but he has. He played me for a fool and killed my lover."

Thomas has no idea Winslow's lover was a man.

"Still, you can't kill this boy. It'll be cold-blooded murder. We're all here to witness."

"Ask me if I care. We're leaving, and you can't stop us because if you try, I'll kill him," Winslow sing-songs over my head. "We're going a—"

Suddenly the voice behind me grunts, goes silent, and the gun falls away from my head as Winslow lets me go. I run to Thomas who reaches out for me, holds me as I turn to see what happened.

Justice takes many forms. A woman filled with revenge, one who has a weapon—a board with a long nail—can deal out a great portion of justice.

Lazarus Winslow lies dead where we stand, a board nailed to the side of his head. His eyes wide, his hands lax, his face contorted in surprise. Behind him, heaving like a winded racehorse, stands Christie Zimmerman, an avenging angel if ever I saw one.

"Jonathan!" she calls out and opens her arms.

Can a person run over a dead man without a thought, straight into the arms of love? For certain! I never miss a step as I high jump over Winslow's body and hurl myself into that woman's embrace. I never want to let go. Home is where she is from now on.

The men help Thomas haul Winslow's body to one side. "We'll take it to the fires," Thomas says bitterly.

Then he and I maneuver Ms. Christie away from that debris mound, her never realizing how close she is to her dead husband.

Only when we return to the house do I tell her why I had to go so fast. What it was Thomas called me to see. She tries to run. Return to the man we found. But it's night, and she can't find her way. I assure her Mr. Jack is no longer there. That Thomas took care of him as gently as Samuel took care of Lawrence. She cries most of the night, scaring the girls who cling to me.

At dawn, Thomas shows up and places something in the palm of my hand. "We never found the boy, but the missus might want this." He jerks the brim of his cap in salute. "God bless, boy."

As the sun rises over the gulf, I place in Christie Zimmerman's hand the gold band she gave Mr. Jack when they married...the ring inscribed like hers.

Forever changed by your love.

THE YEARS FLASH BY

I've stowed my sea bag below deck, checked in with the mate in charge of engineering and now stand on deck, waiting for my family to arrive. Nerves jingle my body. My first time out was a long time coming. But worth the wait as the years passed quick enough.

The railing chills through my tunic. Smoke circles my head as I puff away, a habit even Ms. Christie could never break. My first time away from the family and all I can do is think about them. How Louise is almost ten now. Five-year-old Mattie reminds me of her long-gone brother Jackie. How the family changed on the day Ms. Christie and Tilman Fuller called me into the Zimmerman Boarding House's restored parlor and asked for my blessings to wed. I cried as much as she did. Tilman stood manly by, but I know tears ran down his cheek. I gave Ms. Christie away at the small wedding where the girls scattered flowers down the aisle.

I wept like a baby the day the new Mr. and Mrs. Fuller asked me to be their son...to allow them to adopt me. Big ol' seventeen-year-old me. No greater honor ever fell on me when I became Jonathan Fuller before God and the county judge.

During those years, Ms. Christie leveled the boarding house and re-opened for business. Fuller, of course, came back along with four new boarders. McGraw and Thrill never returned. Winslow was dead as a wedge and never missed. Vassy and Juliet along with their families disappeared in the 1900 storm, as did several of the men who worked in the furniture workshop. Before Ms. Christie married again, the boarding house alone supported her, the girls and me. After that, the income included Mr. Fuller's hardware store.

To the citizens' surprise, the City Council proposed building a seawall to protect Galveston from a storm surge. Even more amazing was the idea of raising the entire city so it lay above sea level. The seawall construction took about eighteen months. No one wanted to put off safety. Ms. Christie, on Tilman's advice (that was before they married), allowed me to sign on to create the wall. To this day, my biggest delight is walking Seawall Boulevard and watching the spray splash up on the wall. A few storms came and went through those years, and I loved watching the waves crash up against the seawall and rise high, only to spill over without wiping out the town.

Even as that project neared completion in early 1904, in December of 1903 the city began its more ambitious project—raising the entire city by barricading off blocks of the city, lifting everything in that area—including all city services—then pumping in sand from the ship channel at the east end of the island. A canal ran down the middle of Galveston, and dredges carried the mixture of sand and water from one end of the island to the area being raised. The only danger came when the giant blowpipes spewed out the mixture. Children liked to run through it. That mixture knocked over more than one.

Even Louise and Mattie got into trouble with the sand mixture. On one of those days when nothing seemed to go right, I was home, having just gotten over a twisted ankle. The next day I was due back on the job. By then, I'd been studying shipping and cargo that ships carry, preparing to take my place aboard a merchant ship when I turned twenty. I promised Ms. Christie I'd wait until life settled. I knew even then that for her, her new husband and children, life would be anything but settled. But I waited.

On that particular day, Ms. Christie moaned that she wished there were three of her. When she discovered that she had no bread to serve for dinner, Louise and Mattie volunteered to walk down the raised sidewalks to the store three blocks away. Ms. Christie gave Louise a small purse and tucked the change for the bread into it. She also warned her oldest daughter to watch the youngest daughter as that little girl had a tendency to get in trouble. I volunteered to go, of course, but the lady of the house ordered me to more manly jobs.

"Be good," I said with a wink to Mattie, knowing that *good* wasn't something she was particularly good at.

Sure enough, not ten minutes later, a young man came running to the house screaming for Ms. Christie. She and I reached the front door at the same time, and she all but screamed, "I can't have a crisis right now...I'm busy!"

But when that fella said, "Your girls have fallen into the dredge sand," she hitched up her skirts and shot out like a flash, me running to keep up. Dredge sand is sand mixed with water. When it's poured, it's like quick sand. You leave it alone, and the water settles out. The sand becomes hard as a rock. But it's that time between *quick sand* and *hard as a rock* that is dangerous. And our little ones were in that mess.

We reached the girls at the same time. "If you reach for one and pull her out, the other will be sucked down," I yelled. Mattie was closet, but Louise was up to her chest by then and further away. "We have to pull at the same time," I yelled to Ms. Christie, hoping that her tiny frame would be strong enough to save her youngest daughter. With my longer arms, I could reach Louise but pulling her out would take all I had.

"On the count of three," Ms. Christie yelled. "One. Two. Three."

We reached out, grabbed at the same time, and hauled back as hard as we could. Just when I thought I might not be strong enough, a pair of hands caught my belt at my back. Someone else had Ms. Christie with arms around her waist. We hauled like our lives depended on it. And fell backwards with two wet and sandy little girls laying on our chests.

After the hugging and crying came the swats. Those two ladies stayed in their rooms several days, standing, as their bottoms were sore.

A grin spreads across my face as I toss my smoke over the side. Those two —I'm gonna miss them and their antics. Mattie is teaching Louise how to take life by the horns and be a stinker. And Louise was a handful to begin with! I don't envy Ms. Christie and Tilman while I'm gone.

Speaking of going, my family's cutting it close. We sail at noon with the tide. No sooner do I think they might not make it to the dock in time than I hear my name.

"Jonathan! Jonathan!" There're my girls: Louise in a bright pink jacket and matching hat and Mattie in a blue coat minus her hat that she probably threw out the window of the car. I rush to meet them, letting the seaman on duty at the gangway know I'll only be a few minutes, then be ready to sail.

"Oh, Jonathan!" Ms. Christie gathers me to her like she's done so many times since I met her five—almost six—years ago now. We've never been apart for more than a day since the great storm of 1900—that's what the weathermen call it. I have other names for it, but none that history will record.

"I don't know if I can let you go," she whispers as she hugs me close.

"I'll come back. Promise."

"Son, I don't know what I'll do without you," Tilman says as he first shakes my hand, then surrenders to emotion and hugs me as well.

"I'll miss y'all, too," I tell him.

"When will you come home, Jonathan?" Mattie wants to know.

"A year from now, darling. You be good while I'm gone. Please," I add, knowing full well that child will be in a ton of mischief before my ship clears the channel.

"Oh, Jonathan, don't go." Louise hugs me so tight that she chokes my neck.

"I have to, sweetheart. I've always wanted to go to sea and help the big ships move cargo. If I don't like it, I promise I'll come home and be a sand crab instead of a lobster." She's been studying those and knows one stays on land and one lives in the sea.

"Okay, but hurry home," she admonishes.

"I've not even left yet!" I say in my squeaky silly voice, pulling my head back and acting all offended. Both girls laugh, while Ms. Christie and Tilman grin. We all know I'm only pulling the little girl's leg. Once more, she gives me a ferocious hug.

Not to be outdone, Mattie joins her sister. Afraid neither of them will let go, I stand carefully, a little girl held in one arm, a larger girl in the other. I lean forward, so Ms. Christie can take Mattie, while I give Louise to her stepfather whom I'm happy to say she adores.

"If I don't go now, I'll miss my ship, and the captain will report me. Give me a kiss and let me go. I'll be back before you know it!"

Kisses all around and I run for the gangplank. Not because I'm late but because my heart threatens to break. I've lost so many in such a few short years. These few are so precious to me.

Still a new life lies ahead of me. Home will always be the boarding house on Avenue L on Galveston island, a city changed forever by a massive storm. As was my life.

EPILOGUE

"It sure did, Jonathan. It sure did." A tall man leans against a cane as he stands at the foot of a grave, the headstone worn but still bearing a name, the dates of birth and death and service to the United States carved into the stone. The sultry air of September eighth beats down on his body, reminding him of days so far in his past they've almost slipped away. But not totally. Never totally gone.

"One day you said the Gulf would swallow me up, then spit me out again. And it did." The man shudders. Almost fearfully, he glances up, noting the clear sky. Weather forecasts call for calm seas and clear skies for the next week. That's the only reason he's come at this time of year... to visit a city that should have died...just as he should have.

"Did you find him, Granddad?" A young woman joins the man. She slips her arm through the crock of his, and they stare at the grave together.

"I did indeed, Julie." Using her for support, he gestures with his cane. "That's my brother, Jonathan. I outlived him, but seems he did pretty well for himself, considering all he went through." He lowers the cane to the ground again, so his granddaughter can bend down and read aloud:

Jonathan Evan Fuller
Born January 4, 1886
Died January 1915
United States Merchantman

"He died in World War I?"

"Yes. Well, before the United States joined in the action. He served on other merchant ships but joined this particular one only a week before it went down. Hit by a German torpedo. I doubt the captain even knew his name yet. He was a merchantman...worked aboard commercial ships that carried goods to England. I understand his original stone was accidently crushed, so the Fullers set up a new one and added that line about being a merchantman."

The man sighs. So much time and he never contacted his brother to say hello...to let Jonathan know he lived.

"You always said you had regrets about Great Uncle Jonathan. Why?"

"He'd like hearing you call him that, sweetheart." George Evans tucks Julie's arm through his once more. He pats her hand with his that trembles more each day.

"So, what happened?"

"I lived through the most horrible experience of my life—well, maybe the second most horrible experience. Losing this leg was the worst experience—took a lot longer to get over than I ever imagined. But Jonathan never knew I survived, and I..." George squirms, an odd gesture for a man in his late seventies.

"What happened, Granddad? Why come to Galveston just to see the grave of someone who died a long time ago?"

Both stare at the grave, transfixed by the stillness inside a cemetery surrounded by busy thoroughfares.

"Jonathan and I came to Galveston from a tiny community that disappeared with time. Our mother died, and our dad abandoned us. My brother was old enough to get a job, and I was only nine. Everyone called me Georgie back then. Jonathan often spoke in funny voices to make us laugh. He'd say my name all squeaky-like. Other kids would roll over laughing."

Julie giggles but motions her grandfather to continue.

"I finagled a way to stay with the Catholic sisters at St. Mary's orphanage. No one said I was an orphan exactly, but when it came to meals and a bed, the sisters took care of me. Unlike the others, however, I could come and go as I pleased as long as I did the chores Sister set me to. Several times a week, I'd ride to town with one of the sisters and find Jonathan. He worked in various places until he started working for a man named Zimmerman. 'Mr. Jack' everyone called him. Nice man. Eventually he worked for Mr. Jack's wife, Ms. Christie, at the boarding house. The house took in railroad men when they were between trains, coming and going. They took in others, too." He leans against the top of his cane, one hand tucked into his pocket, going back decades in his mind.

"I remember the Christmas of 1899. Jonathan told Mr. Jack and his wife that the only ones of his friends he trusted to come into their home and not hurt anyone or bother anything were me and Samuel." George stops, a smile lighting his face. "Samuel," he tells his granddaughter, "was a black boy, about Jonathan's age...maybe a year or so older. Don't know how it happened, but we three wound up best friends. Anyway, Ms. Christie invited Samuel and me to the house the day before Christmas Eve. She knew the nuns wouldn't let me go anywhere Christmas Eve or Christmas day. Samuel said his family went to church the night before Christmas and had friends over for Christmas day, so she asked us over. You should have seen the tree in the front parlor. We sang holiday songs, and Vassy the cook made us a special dinner, just for me, Samuel and Jonathan. Of course, the family all had a finger in the doings. Just before Sister came for me, Ms. Christie called us back into the parlor and pulled out two packages for me and two for Samuel. She told Jonathan he'd have to wait until Christmas morning. I was never so surprised in all my life! Samuel looked like the earth opened up and was about to swallow him, he was so shocked." George stops and grins, nodding.

"What'd you get?" Julie asks, tugging on his arm to get her grandfather to finish the Christmas story.

"Well, let me think. I got a sweater and a cap like Jonathan's. Certainly, a lot warmer than that threadbare jacket I'd been wearing. Samuel got a cap as well, but he got a new neck scarf. His coat was still good, but he often walked home, and the wind went right down his neck. He'd said that more than once. The scarf he wore was thin and had holes in it. Not a lot of protection. Ms. Christie was one smart lady. She listened. Eventually Sister showed up, and I drove off with her, but not before giving that lady a big kiss and shaking hands with Mr. Jack. Samuel was so shy he couldn't think of what to do, so Ms. Christie hugged him, while Mr. Jack shook his hand. Best Christmas ever!"

"You say that every Christmas, Granddad!"

"You don't understand, Julie. That Christmas was my first. As much as our mother tried to have a special day with gifts, we just didn't have the means, and our father wasn't one to stop working or whatever he was doing in order to dally away a day for some man who was born in a manger. I'll remember that day as long as I live. That was the first time I felt like I was worth something to someone besides my brother. And even then, the Zimmermans didn't know Jonathan and I were related. They did it because we were his friends, and they liked us. A kindness of the heart, you could say."

"What happened to that boy, Samuel?"

"Have no idea. I suppose he was one of those who didn't survive the storm." By now, George feels a familiar nagging fatigue coming on.

"According to the ancestry information I found, Mr. Jack and his oldest son didn't either. That boy Jackie and I used to play together when we came to visit Jonathan. He was a rounder, that one. Records do show the youngest died the day after the storm. Ms. Christie...well, Mrs. Fuller years later...lived a long life. Even outlived her second husband. They never had children. I always thought that odd. But the girls, Louise and Mattie, married and had large families. Strange how tangled that hunt was to find Jonathan through the maze of records. I'm glad you talked me into looking."

Tired now, George slumps. His leg pains him just enough to be noticed, and the radiation treatments he's taken leaves him perpetually worn out. Not far from his brother's grave is a stone bench. He again gestures with his cane. "Let's sit a little while, and I'll rest a bit."

They move slowly to the bench, Julie helping him ease down, then sitting close.

"Sounds like tough times, Granddad," she remarks.

"That's not real subtle, young lady." George lands a gentle punch to her arm. "You just want to hear the rest of the story."

"Well, yeah. I mean, I'm a writer, so why not."

"You're in college and *want* to be a writer. There's a difference, my girl."

"I guess you'd know," Julie admits. "After all, you went to college when no one thought you'd make it 'cause of your leg, and you became a writer for the biggest newspaper in the state."

"Too true, and don't you forget it."

"Whatever this story is, you need to write it. You know?" Julie reflects.

"You've not even heard it yet," George retorts.

"It's about you, Granddad, and you've lived an exciting life."

George glances around at the beauty and peace of the place—the final resting place for so many—since that fateful day. The people who died in September 1900 don't rest here though. Another sigh escapes him.

"Come on. Before you get too sad to talk about it. Tell me the rest of the story."

"Not much to tell really. I returned to the orphanage with Sister that day, September 8, 1900. I thought we'd never get to the place. Galveston Island was getting hit harder than anyone could remember. The weather had gone wild. Back then we had no idea a hurricane could touch the island. Sister kept mumbling, but eventually I couldn't even hear her over the rain pounding us so hard. The kids at the orphanage grew afraid. But the sisters assured us nothing bad would happen. We even sang a song, Queen of the Waves." In his mind, George returns to that day, to the water rising, the waves tossing life around as if each one was a matchstick. With a mammoth effort, he shakes off haunting memories and refocuses on his granddaughter, a child with fair skin, warm brown hair, a sweet smile and eyes like emeralds. For the first time, he realizes why he's so fond of this particular child.

"You look like him, you know. I just realized that."

"Really? I look like your brother? Cool."

"It's like having a part of him back again," George admits and hugs her arm closer.

Silence falls between them until Julie gets restless and digs a gentle elbow into her grandfather's side. "The story," she reminds him.

"Okay, here goes. Jonathan was in town with the Zimmermans. They had taken him in to live there. He wanted to let them know about me—ask if I could live with them, too—but the family was big already, and Ms. Christie had had her fourth child that winter. I told him life was good as it was, and when I was a little older I'd try to get a job with Mr. Zimmerman—Mr. Jack—so we'd be close all the time." George shifts his weight. He's lost a lot of weight recently and hasn't as much padding on his rear as he used to.

"Mr. Jack's workshop was down the street from the boarding house. Must have been half dozen men or more worked for him. All excellent furniture makers. His work was well-known on the island. All of it washed away by that storm though." He pauses to remember the Zimmerman family, those so good to his brother. "Anyway, life rocked along, and we often played on the beach. I tempted the waves by running up to them, then running back up on the beach, so the water wouldn't get me. I didn't want to ride in wet clothes back with the sister. The orphanage was a few miles from the center of town. That day—September 8—the weather was foul. There wasn't such a thing as instant weather updates like there are now. No one had any idea an enormous hurricane was headed our way. The whole town pretty much sat at beach level, so when waves rose higher and higher, I knew those near the beach would be washed away. That's what the reports said and all the books I've read since then. At St Mary's orphanage, we huddled together, then moved higher and higher in the dormitory to escape rising water. The sisters tied the little ones together with clothesline, then to themselves, but I hid, afraid I'd be swept away if something happened to the one I was tethered to. As happened."

Julie gasped. "You were there? But your name isn't among the dead."

"Obviously! Because I didn't die that day," George teases her.

"Granddad! You know what I mean. The dead were listed and the survivors, but your name's not anywhere." She grows quiet. "No wonder your brother thought you were dead...simply lost at sea."

"Exactly. The sisters never entered my name on the roster because I wasn't even supposed to be there. When the building collapsed, and all were lost, I got swept up by the waves and carried for miles as far as I can remember. Buried under debris for several days across the bay, I'm surprised I lived at all. Then, of course, I was ill for so long after that primitive operation that took my leg." He waved his cane in the air. "I'm surprised I even remembered my name when I woke up. By then, Doctor Warren and his family were on the train headed back to Iowa—with me. The first thing I can remember is someone asking if I had any family. I must have mumbled that they were dead—as I thought Jonathan was. So, the Warrens up and took me home with them."

"And you grew up with them. They never adopted you, did they?"

"No. I asked them not to. As the last Evans, I felt it was my duty to carry the name forward." He tickles Julie on her arm. "And I'm glad I did. Nana Evans and I had two great sons, and they have lovely families—all named Evans." He grins and nods to the grave across the wide asphalt path. "I think Jonathan would have liked that."

"You never came back to find him?"

"I thought he was dead, sweetheart, like thousands were after that day. It just seemed a waste of time. History refers to that day as the 1900 storm that wiped out Galveston, Texas. With all the homes destroyed and six thousand or more dead, I honestly didn't think Jonathan and the Zimmermans survived. You're the one who got me to investigate Jonathan and see what happened. Surprise! Surprise! His trail didn't end in 1900 like I thought. He survived! Like Galveston did."

"But you still had to find out what happened to him," Julie continued for him.

"I looked for Evans, but no one by that name was listed as dead, and no one was listed by that name that lived. What was I to think? Who knew Mr. Jack died and Ms. Christie remarried a man named Fuller who adopted my brother. I had to be a detective to track down all that information. Lots of paper work, let me tell you!" George lets out an exaggerated breath of air as if he's just finished a long race.

"But you did it! And here we are. Celebrating Great Uncle Jonathan's life."

"*Celebrating*—that's a good way to put it. I like that. Yes, I do."

They sit and watch gulls fly across the final resting place of so many. Finally, sunlight fades, leaving headstones in shadows and mausoleums in silhouettes.

"Come on, young lady. Time to say goodbye to Jonathan. I did what I came to do. Tell him I survived. That the sea swallowed me up, then spit me out to a better life than I ever imagined...or probably deserved."

"Granddad, don't talk like that," Julie whispers as she helps him stand.

They move back across the pathway and stop one last time before the grave. Julie walks off, giving her grandfather privacy. George makes his way carefully to the headstone and lays a wrinkled sun-spotted hand on the warm granite.

"Bye, Jonathan. I love you." He rubs the stone one last time, then steps back. Before turning to join Julie, he gives his brother one last nod. "I miss you every day. Farewell, big brother. We'll meet again soon. Very soon."

AUTHOR'S NOTE

I was born on Galveston Island. My father's family lived there as did my mother's, though neither were born there. BOI is how we true-born islanders describe ourselves—Born On the Island.

My mother's family lived in Galveston before the 1900 storm. I grew up hearing stories about the family and what happened to them during that wild weekend. Some of those stories are woven into this novel.

Evans was the name of a family friend—a merchant seaman. He's long gone now, but he and my great-aunt Mildred shared a home for many years after he gave up the sea.

Aunt Mildred never married. She was less than a year old when the great storm hit the island. Her parents did indeed work with wood and own a boarding house. They survived, but I'm not sure if they stayed in the house or went to higher ground. The checker table that Mr. Jack made for Ms. Christie in this novel is real. My grandmother gave it to my dad, and Mom gave it to me. At one time, when I was a kid, the imprint of a tiny pair of embroidery scissors could be seen in one corner of the top. The story about the little girls caught in the dredge sand is real. That would be little Mattie playing the part of Aunt Mildred. The names *Jack* and *Christie* are family names.

The story of St. Mary's Orphanage collapsing and all the nuns and children drowning, but for three older boys, is true. There is a historical plaque on the Sea Wall showing where the orphanage stood. Also true is the death cart details, the men attending those carts almost exclusively Negros.

I wrote this novel in twenty-one days in November 2016, during National Novel Writing Month (referred to as NaNoWriMo). Those few days don't include the six weeks of intensive research I put in preparing to write. As I read one book after another and followed trails on the Internet, what amazed me was that the loss of lives in the city of Galveston and the rest of the island that weekend could have been prevented or drastically minimized if not for squabbles between noted weathermen. One suspected a huge storm was coming—the man who lived on the island, while another in Washington DC deliberately put out misinformation indicating the storm was headed to Florida and the Atlantic. Blame comes with hindsight. Too late for that. But Galveston recovered and took measures to prevent a repeat of the 1900 storm catastrophe. Hurricanes Alicia in 1983, Ike in 2008 and Harvey in 2017 tested the strength not only of the island's defenses but the people as well.

If needed someday, I hope I have that kind of will to survive and come back stronger.

ABOUT THE AUTHOR

In humid beautiful Texas one hundred miles from the Gulf of Mexico, I have been an educator, Challenge Course facilitator, photographer, security staff and now a writer. Wife, mother and grandmother. These titles fit me well. I've held them all--some far longer than others. The title I long strived for was that of writer—now published author.

As a writer, my imagination creates whatever I want. Once I've written something I want to share, it is time to edit, hone that manuscript until there is no doubt what I want the reader to experience. I'm still working at that. And always will. Any writer who says, "I've got this down pat," is only fooling herself.

There are no rules to what your imagination comes up with, but there are guidelines to follow if you want that story to be the best it can. So, writers are also learners. Constantly attending conferences, taking classes, reading, communicating with fellow writers. The trick is to take what you learn and make it your own. Write in a way that no one else does. Be fresh!

There is no new story—each has been told. The idea is to tell your story in a new way. So, we fill notebooks with ideas, pages with storybook names, jot down dire circumstances then one day, we the writers, pull out an idea from here and a name from there and put it all together. We add tension, conflict, danger, doubt, suspense and maybe love if that's your thing. Polish the words and craft them until you have a story that begs to be read and enjoyed.

That is my challenge: to write such a story. I strive toward that goal every day.

Enjoy...
Jane Carver
(also writing as Elizabeth Eden and Ruth Bolin)

http://janiecarver2011@wordpress.com

ALSO BY JANE CARVER

Satin Romance

Winning The Ranger's Heart in *Western Ways Anthology*

Fire & Ice Young Adult Books

(as Jane Grace)

Until I'm Safe

Ghosts In My Soul